My Biscuit Baby

My Biscuit Baby

See you at Pig Farm!,
John Bare
Dec. 2023

JOHN BARE

A LASSIE JAMES MYSTERY

My Biscuit Baby

Published by Wisdom House Books, Inc.
Chapel Hill, North Carolina 27517 USA
www.wisdomhousebooks.com

Wisdom House Books is committed to excellence in the publishing industry.
Book design copyright © 2024 by Wisdom House Books, Inc.
All rights reserved.

Cover and Interior Design by Ted Ruybal
Published in the United States of America

Paperback ISBN: 978-1-7349884-8-2
eBook ISBN: 978-1-7349884-4-4
LCCN: 2023919327

1. FIC022000 | FICTION / Mystery & Detective / General
2. FIC022100 | FICTION / Mystery & Detective / Amateur Sleuth
3. FIC027110 | FICTION / Romance / Suspense

First Edition

25 24 23 22 21 20 / 10 9 8 7 6 5 4 3 2 1

For Joe Mitchell

This is a work of fiction.

Only the biscuits are real.

Contents

Chapter One

WEDNESDAY MORNING, OCTOBER 2ND

Hortense Barbee inserted a forefinger and pinky in the corners of her mouth and whistled loud enough to hush the crowd.

"What a glorious day to take back our land from the government!" she shouted.

Fans chanted. *Doll. Doll. Doll.* Everybody called her Doll. Nobody called her Hortense.

"She might as well light gas cans and toss them down," I said to Siler.

Her fans cheered. Protestors screamed. Doll raised her arms to the Chapel Hill sky.

She was twenty feet in the air, alongside the western corner of Gimghoul Road and Glandon Drive spilling into Battle Park.

Doll's polling numbers had been climbing ever since she started rolling the bucket truck into towns and speaking from the perch. She parked her workingman's vehicle by million-dollar homes and dared the tight-asses to expel her.

I was leaning on a bitternut hickory tree. Green leaves with edges showing Klimt gold. Siler stood beside me. He shifted his weight and scratched the trail dirt with a stick. He shook his head.

"The Cabins at Battle Park and The Battle Branch Distillery will bring this old land alive," Doll shouted into a megaphone, her voice rattling the leaves. "When the government hoards land, we all lose. When we expand private ownership of land, the economy booms and we all win. New homes and new jobs and new whiskey right here in these woods. And a billion dollars to help working families pay tuition to the University."

"So?" Siler asked.

He used the stick to scratch a question mark in the trail dirt and the toe of his Keen boot to add the dot. We stood a few yards into the Battle Park woods, just past the benches at Sisters' Corner, on the edge of 93 acres of unspoiled forest. Sacred ground. Now being sold to developers funding Doll's campaign. A one-billion-dollar windfall for the seller, the University of North Carolina.

"I think she's got a shot," I replied. "Governor Doll? You ready for that?"

The day brought an unclouded sky. Against it, the white Dur-A-Lift bucket shimmered. Same with Doll's smile and her romper. She'd taken to wearing white outfits at rallies. All the better to draw attention to her signature gold scarf. The accessory featuring blood-red lettering. T H A I. The signifier for the new third party, Tar Heels Against Immigration, seeking to elect Doll governor.

"Forget the nanny state Dems! Forget the country club Republicans!" Doll shouted into the megaphone. "On November 5th, order THAI!"

The three-way race was bunched up. No way to predict a winner. Emelyn Wheeler, whom everybody called Miss Emmy, was the Republican incumbent. Signs for Miss Emmy's Barbecue Shacks spackled the state's highways, drawing travelers to restaurants she'd situated at 51 interstate exits. Her pig farms scented Sampson County. The Democratic challenger, Dr. Janie Spearman, held another statewide office, state superintendent of public instruction. She'd been a celebrated math professor at Howard University and UNC-Greensboro before entering politics. Doll's commercial real estate development firm, based in Kinston, had strip malls in 41 of the state's 100 counties.

"Bulldozing Developer vs. BBQ Queen vs. Mathematician," according to the newspaper headline writers.

A white Suburban SUV crept down Gimghoul Road. It stopped behind the bucket truck. Its windows tinted dark as a root cellar.

From the curbside door emerged Stokes Avery wearing a suit the shade of mile-deep ocean water. Silver pinstripes danced. THAI scarf hung off his neck. From the opposite door stepped Cornelia Sloop. She wore black denim jeans and a puffy pirate blouse. With one hand, she waved her THAI scarf in the air. She held a bottle of champagne in the other.

"Sweet couple," Siler said. He tossed the stick into the ancient woods and picked up his thermos of coffee from a stump. Steam escaped when he dialed open the lid.

Corn Stalks. Corn Stalks. Corn Stalks. Doll's fans chanted the nickname for the power couple, which doubled as the name of their commercial real estate development concern.

With the General Assembly's appointments of Cornelia and Stokes to the University's Board of Trustees, the THAI supporters secured a 7-6 voting edge. The majority was expected to greenlight the University's sale of Battle Park to Corn Stalks. The developers promised a makeover. What Siler called an evisceration. Doll made the deal the centerpiece of her campaign. Making good on her promise to scrape the ivory off the University.

Siler swallowed more boiling coffee. He looked at me and raised his eyebrows.

"Trustees vote next week," I said. "The 11th. Day before University Day."

Every October 12th for the past 150 years, the University has celebrated the anniversary of the laying of the cornerstone of Old East Dorm, the oldest building at the oldest public university in the country.

Doll was back on the megaphone.

"Friends," Doll shouted, "please give a THAI welcome to Stokes Avery and Cornelia Sloop. They are here to christen The Cabins at Battle Park and The Battle Branch Distillery."

From the Dur-A-Lift truck, speakers spat out a hissing recording of a drum roll, which gave way to a hissing recording of "Boot Scootin' Boogie."

"Hey, you, get off of my tree," Cornelia said to me as the couple approached. She was dancing her way into the park.

Doll's fans chanted. Cornelia was eyeing my bitternut hickory. She was winding up and taking exaggerated practice swings with the champagne bottle. I stepped around Siler and the tree stump Siler was using for a coffee table. Stepped away from the bitternut. At first, I doubted a blow to the tree would break the bottle. Then again, Corn Stalks would have the show business worked out. For sure, they must have a crushable prop bottle for Cornelia to shatter.

"Pearl?" Siler said.

"She's at home," I said.

I was looking toward the bitternut and watching Corn Stalks shimmy as Doll cheered.

Siler, I saw, was facing away from the tree, looking toward the street, toward his house on Gimghoul Road.

"Pearl," he said again. This time a statement, not a question.

Siler reached out and touched my shoulder.

4

I saw her.

Pearl was stepping off the path and onto the street, by now nearly under Doll's bucket.

She walked with the posture of an athlete. Her gait showed off her swimmer's shoulders. She wore a platinum dress, scuffed black boots, a black jacket and long black gloves. Her boots held onto tan and gold flecks from the dirt path. The distinctive color of Chapel Hill Gravel formed a glitter on her boots and reminded me of another morning walk we took on this street.

"I've seen her wear that before," I said.

"I'm not looking at her clothes," Siler said.

"Yeah," I said, my mind retrieving the recollection. "That's what she wore to her dad's burial service last year. We walked down this street together to the graveside service. That's what she wore."

"Well. She's added flair," Siler said.

Then it came into view. The long barrel of the shotgun. Pearl was across the blacktop now and stepping onto the dirt and leaves. All eyes in the crowd were on the bitternut and the dancing Corn Stalks.

"Could you have her shoot out the speakers before she shoots Corn Stalks?" Siler said.

"How do we stop this?" I said.

"Looks like Pearl is on her way to stopping this," Siler said.

Sudden silence. The hissing and scootin' stopped. The Dur-A-Lift dee-jay saw Pearl, finally.

"That .410 was lost," Siler said to me. Pearl was past the benches and alongside us both.

"Now it's found," Pearl said.

Corn Stalks stood between Pearl and the bitternut. When the scootin' stopped, they turned to look. They froze.

I held still. Doll's fans fell silent. Protestors, too. I could hear a thin squeak. The bolts holding Doll's bucket to the telescoping arm.

"Pearl," I said. "Pearl. I love you."

"Lassie," Stokes said. His voice was low. A tick above a whisper. "Get hold of your wife, goddammit. Get that gun away from her." Spit hung on his lower lip.

Cornelia dropped the bottle. It hit the leaves and broke apart. A prop bottle, for sure.

Siler shook his head.

"Cornelia," Pearl said, "get out of here."

Cornelia looked at her husband. Cornelia looked back at Pearl. She stood still.

"Leave. Get the fuck out, Cornelia," Pearl said. "Now."

Cornelia held both ends of her THAI scarf and ran to the SUV. The truck drove off.

A portion of Doll's fans fled on foot. Another segment of her fanbase watched in silence. Others held up their phones to record the events.

"Lassie," Stokes said. "Lassie, some help here, man."

"This is your show," I said. "You don't like the new script, you better take it up with Pearl."

"Face the tree," Pearl said to Stokes.

The developer turned away from Pearl. His suit swallowed him. Silver pinstripes sagged. On the back of his neck where clipped gray hairs touched his white collar, Pearl placed the end of the shotgun.

"Pearl," I said. "Call it a win. Let's live to fight another day. Pearl, I love you."

Pearl pushed the shotgun into his nape until the force required him to take a step forward. Then another. Then another. His chest was flush against the bitternut.

Pearl shoved the shotgun harder. His nose crunched against the bark.

"Kiss the tree," she said. "You wanna kill these trees? This tree? Show me something. Kiss this tree. Tell this tree why you want to kill it. Tell this tree why you believe your life is worth more than its life."

"Pearl," Siler said. "Give me my shotgun."

Pearl stabbed the gun barrel harder into Stokes's neck. Blood ran from his nose.

"For me, it's an easy call," Pearl said. "This tree has done more for the world than you'll ever do. You think it's killing season? OK. You're first in line. You ready to give your life so your wife can come back and kill this tree?"

The wind blew. Tree limbs squirmed. Sounds of moving air drowned out the squeak from Doll's bucket bolts.

A bitternut leaf edged with autumn fell to rest on Pearl's left shoulder, opposite the shoulder bracing the shotgun.

Pearl blinked. The bitternut was talking to her. She adored these woods. The trees talked to her. On the boiling August days, when air was thick as gravy, the trees told her about the secret places in Battle

Park that held on to the cool. In January, when leaves underfoot made Rice Krispies sounds, the trees told her where to find sunbeams. Once when I was sleepless at 3 a.m., I heard her whispering prayers in her sleep. In bed beside her, I listened. Later, when I asked her about what I observed, she said the trees visited her in her dreams and taught her prayers. As she told me this, she reached out and touched my right cheek with the back of her right hand. I felt electricity in my bones.

With Stokes pinned to the tree, Pearl blinked again. A tear dripped from her cheekbone.

She pulled the gun barrel out of Stokes's neck. She flipped the .410 into the air. The long gun spun half a revolution. Gravity cooperated. With two hands, Pearl caught it by the barrel. In the same motion, she turned her upper body to the right, as Cornelia had done practicing her champagne swing. Pearl whipped the long gun forward, swiveling her hips to jack up the force at the moment the stock of the shotgun cracked against Stokes's ribs. Air left his lungs. Stokes fell face-first into the trail dirt. He filled his suit trousers with piss.

Pearl flipped the shotgun in the air. Another long half-turn. She snagged it cleanly again. She propped the gun on her shoulder. Like a drill team member in the marching band, Pearl walked back to Siler's house. Her head held high.

The bucket bolts squealed as Doll's conveyer hiccupped, signaling the start of her descent.

A man rushed past me heading toward campus.

"Call me," he said.

Chapter Two

WEDNESDAY EVENING, OCTOBER 2ND

*P**lease release me . . .* Ray Price sang from the Klipsch Heresy speakers Siler found in an abandoned storage locker he bought, sight unseen. Siler stamped 1957 on the wood veneers and told everyone he'd snatched from the dumpster genuine vintage speakers from the first lot Klipsch ever produced.

We were in Siler's bar, Pig Farm Tavern in Chapel Hill. Less than a mile from this morning's row.

"Too soon," I said.

Siler shrugged. "It was either that or 'My Felon Girlfriend,'" he said.

I worked the app on my phone and queued up Lucinda Williams and Wilco tunes on the juke.

"Can't believe he hasn't called me back yet," I said.

"Watched pot," Siler said, directing his eyes to my phone to remind me that staring at it wouldn't make it ring.

He poured more genmaicha tea into my mug. Steam curled around the kettle's spout. A glass beside it contained fresh ice and Bulleit Rye.

"So what exactly did he say when he ran by you this morning?" Siler asked.

"He said 'Call me,'" I said. "Then poof. He was gone."

By the time I caught up with Pearl in front of Siler's house down the street from Battle Park on Gimghoul Road, cops were there. She was in cuffs. The lady cop was pushing Pearl's head down to squeeze her into the back seat. Pearl smiled at me through the car window. Put her lips together to make a kiss. Touched her forehead against the window, the way she touches her forehead to mine. She talks to me with her eyes that way, explains the past to me. Tells me the future will be OK.

"They really do that, pushing the head into the car door," I said. "I thought the head push was a movie thing."

Jeff Tweedy was dreaming of California stars. Siler listened.

"I followed the cop car to the jail. Left a voice mail for him on the way," I said. "Tried to bribe the jailer but couldn't get in to see Pearl. Called him again on the way here."

"Then you called him from here about every hour asking about Pearl," Siler said.

Behind the bar, Siler was in the position. Leaning his right elbow on the bar. Coffee in his left hand. More curiosity in his eyes than usual. Too interesting a day for the usual dumb look. He put the last bite of a pimento cheese sandwich into his mouth and rubbed his hands together to shed crumbs. He found his whiskey glass empty and the Bulleit bottle empty. He used a wood-handle knife to cut the seal on a new bottle.

"Lassie James!" a voice shot out of the stairwell. We heard the voice before a head cleared the landing and came into view.

Argus Tooley Peppers was a lousy bass player and a witty lawyer. He was a Connor Dorm friend back in the early 1980s. One day into the unair-condi-

10

tioned August orientation, he became Ghost. The name stuck. Siler, Ghost and I found adventure on the dorm's second floor. For our Wednesday evening cookouts, Ghost threw frozen meat out the hall's south window to Siler, who ran the grill below. On the early morning walks from Franklin Street bars back to the dorm, he'd let out a scream and sprint toward a hedge of hollies or boxwoods. At the last split-second, Ghost would halt. The others, following their fearless Ghost, leapt head-first into the shrubs. The thickets welcomed flesh as cutlery would. If the shrubbery didn't stop the divers, the brick walkway on the other side always did.

Ghost was the bass player in our dorm band, Snow Camp. Delaney-Quinn, guitar and vocals. Pre-med back then, now she's a gastroenterologist in Raleigh. H.F. Turley on lead vocals. He had been a speech major. Now he's farming trout and Christmas trees in the mountains. In the town of Sparta, I believe. Siler and I split time driving the van. We held our dinner meetings at The Porthole. Whenever we could score tickets, we'd head out to see a show at the Cradle or The Pier. Fabulous Knobs or Pressure Boys or Glass Moon. Then we'd end up in the Connor Dorm basement or any rehearsal room we could snag. The band struggled to keep time. Bunch of different guys on drums. Never did find a drummer. Or maybe the right drummer never found Snow Camp.

"Pour me one, Siler," Ghost said. He took a spot two barstools down from me. "Any sandwiches left?"

From the cooler, Siler pulled a pimento cheese sandwich. Sourdough bread wrapped in butcher paper. For regulars, Siler stocked sandwiches from a local diner, Philpot Lane. He poured a rye. Ghost held up his hand to wave off the ice.

"You gotta return calls," I said.

"An unqualified failure," Ghost hollered. He drank the glass dry and waved

Siler to pour another. "At returning phone calls, I am a disgrace. At this moment, I don't know the whereabouts of my bloody phone. Lawyering was more fun before Steve Jobs fucked up the world."

You can't rule me . . . Lucinda filled up the speakers.

"I do, however, know Pearl's whereabouts. I just left her," Ghost said.

Right off, Ghost said, Pearl was booked on two misdemeanors. Assault by pointing a gun. And communicating threats.

"We can work with that," I said.

"Hold on, Lassie James," Ghost said, swallowing pimento cheese and sourdough and sour mash all together.

Ghost explained that the DA had added a charge of felonious assault with a deadly weapon with intent to kill. That could be a 15-year hitch. That's why she's in the jailhouse tonight and not here.

"Gotta work out terms of release tomorrow morning," Ghost said.

Pig Farm was quiet. I could hear the ice melt in my glass. I worked the phone app. Put on Pearl's favorites from Arlo Guthrie and David Olney.

Olney's voice came out of the speakers first, *Mister Rat and Mister Flea ...*

Nobody said anything for a bit. Ghost interrupted the absence of conversation. "And I was sorry to hear about your parents, Lassie," he said. "Still remember them delivering care packages to the dorm. Never had a better cheese straw than the ones your mom delivered. Woman worked magic with an extruder. Special people, both of 'em."

A decade ago, Mom and Dad moved from Saluda, North Carolina, to Ukraine to serve as missionaries for a progressive, faith-based organization delivering human services and saving girls from being sold into the sex trade.

"Yeah, I was worried the virus would get them," I said. "Putin got them first. Fucked-up world."

"They in the ground over there or over here?" Ghost asked.

"Saluda," I said. "As much red tape as you'd imagine."

"Fuck," Ghost said.

"Hey, thank you, man," I said. "I'm making my peace with it. I was lucky to have them around for 80 years. Crazy luck they were still fighting to the end."

"I mean, fuck, I have more bad news," Ghost said.

Siler woke up. Dumb look dissolving. Curiosity in its place.

Before I could ask, Ghost assured us the forthcoming bad news was not about Pearl.

Ghost had an update on H.F., our old dormmate and front man for Snow Camp.

H.F. was dead.

"Died yesterday," Ghost said. "Heart burst as he was splitting wood. Burst on the downswing. Fell into woodchips. Left a Ludell maul stuck in a sweetgum log."

H.F. had stayed in touch with Ghost over the years. He had Ghost draft his will and handle his estate planning. H.F. directed that, upon his death, his mountain acreage should be transferred to members of the Eastern Band of Cherokee Indians.

"H.F. wrote in his will, 'It was theirs first,'" Ghost said.

"I can still see H.F. singing that biscuit song at Springfest," Siler said.

"Yeah," I said. "First time I ever heard words I wrote turned into a song."

We all sipped a toast to H.F.

"Funny you should say that," Ghost said. "Lassie, this is where you come in."

I leapt in to explain I didn't want anything from H.F.'s estate. Whatever he left me could be directed to a charity or another friend. Or whatever Ghost worked out. Mom and Dad gone. Pearl in jail. All coming after the murder of Pearl's Dad, Dr. Sanders Mallette, the man who'd been my friend and mentor and a beloved University professor. I was past my limit. Past my capacity to give another damn.

"H.F. didn't leave you a thing, Lassie," Ghost said. "No, no, he didn't. He made an ask."

From Siler's old speakers, Arlo was singing about a pickle. I put my face down on the bar.

"So you really plucked these speakers from a storage unit?" Ghost asked. "I remember something like them from the old days. Maybe that rich kid in the dorm. Kid from Charleston. Did he have Klipsch speakers in his room?"

"These are original '57s," Siler said. "You've never seen anything like these."

The cold surface felt good on my forehead. The touch of Pearl's forehead to mine flashed through my brain. Last night, I'd fallen asleep with her forehead touching mine. Felt safe. Pearl's touch always made the world safe for me. The cold surface of the bar wasn't going to cut it.

"Lassie," Ghost said, getting back on track, "H.F. asked that you produce his memorial service. A memorial service in Forest Theatre. Yep, right there in Battle Park. And he requested special music. He wants you to find a band to play songs from the Snow Camp setlist, from that Springfest show."

I heard Siler laugh.

"Fuck me. Impossible. Can't be done," I said.

"What, you just said you remembered writing the biscuit song," Ghost said.

"Yeah, I remember I tried to write some lyrics about a biscuit," I said. "That's it. I don't remember the words. I don't know the music. I don't even know the title. I can't sing. I can't play an instrument."

Everybody fell quiet. My brain ran away to a daydream. More and more these days, I was dreaming awake. Ever since I lost Mom and Dad. Head back down on the bar, my mind carried me to the Olmsted Overlook at Great Falls, Maryland. I was standing tippy-toes on the edge of the cliff. The Potomac chasing itself through the gorge. Down below, I could see Pearl climbing the rocks. No rope. No carabiners. No shoes. Climbing with bare hands and feet, wearing overalls the golden-orange color of a free-range egg yolk. I could see wings on her shoulders. As she cleared the top edge of the cliff, I reached to hold her hand. Then I fell. My fingers missed hers by the width of a slice of country ham. Never felt her touch. As I fell, I could see her remove her wings and toss them to me.

"Lassie, Lassie," Ghost said. "Sorry about the H.F. news. This isn't the time. I should have held that headline to myself. The lawyer in me got out ahead of the friend in me. We'll pick that up later. That's news for another day. For now, know that Pearl's first appearance is in the morning. One thing at a time."

Siler made a face that indicated a question.

Ghost explained that Pearl saw a magistrate today. Ghost was ahead of the cops this morning and at the courthouse waiting when cops rolled up with Pearl. Ghost walked her through the encounter with the magistrate and her booking into county jail.

"She'll enter a plea tomorrow morning?" Siler asked.

"No, at the arraignment. Later," Ghost said. "At the first appearance tomorrow, a District Court judge will review charges, make sure she knows what's what. Ten minutes. In and out. If she were solo, the judge would figure out counsel. That's handled. Two big items tomorrow. First is setting a date for a probable cause hearing. Then the DA will have to decide whether to take it to a grand jury and get an indictment or use the probable cause hearing to bind the case over to Superior Court."

"Second thing?" I asked.

"Bail," Ghost said.

By spirit and statute, the purpose of bail is to secure the accused's appearance at trial. In practice, prosecutors use pre-trial detention punitively. They imprison people before they get their day in court. They use it to turn up the dials to induce a confession. Jail is a miserable fucking place. Bad enough for convicts. For people innocent before proven guilty, it's hell on earth.

"Just between us friends," I said. "A few hundred people saw Pearl do the thing. Most recorded it with cell phones."

"Awww, fuck people. Fuck phones," Ghost said. "You think a jury is gonna believe a few hundred people with computer chips? Or believe me?"

"Any word on the judge?" I asked.

Ghost laughed. He waved Siler over for another pour.

An old David Olney track made it to the top of the queue. *My baby's gone, she's left me here alone.* Siler rapped his knuckles on the bar keeping time with Olney's beat. I started to ask him why he didn't step in long ago to drum for Snow Camp.

"Best intel from the clerks, it's R&R," Ghost said. "Should be a hoot."

Judge Robert Roberts grew up in Goldsboro, the son of an arsonist who hired himself out to torch tobacco warehouses. Owners started out using him in years when they calculated they could make more in insurance money than from their commerce. The warehouse owners eventually kept him on the payroll alongside their legit staff. If they didn't keep him on salary, they feared he'd burn down their places at an inconvenient moment. Daddy Roberts, every owner figured out, was going to burn down a tobacco warehouse at some point. He was born to it. It was in the self-interest of the owners that they determine where and when. They didn't want to see flames in years their businesses flourished.

In mixed company, if asked, Daddy Roberts introduced himself as "an oil & gas man." On his passing, the NC Museum of History added a set of Daddy Roberts's coveralls to an exhibit. The "Roberts Oil & Gas Co." logo on the right breast. R&R, the handle his son carried from birth, grew into Pentecostal preacher and lawyer. R&R always said the Bible was just one more law book. Once the people of Wayne County elected him to the District Court bench, he ran unopposed in every election for four decades. Retired now to a dairy farm in Orange County, he served as a fill-in judge to handle overflow in Chapel Hill and Durham.

"Reminds me of 'Pineola,'" Siler said, tilting his head in my direction as a request for me to queue up the Lucinda song.

"R&R it is, then," I said.

A couple of customers emerged from the stairs. They bought drinks at the bar and settled in at the pool table. I could hear the cue strikes behind me.

"Hey, what did Joansie think of the circus this morning?" I asked.

Joansie and Ghost had been married twenty-something years. An environmental lawyer, Joansie held the top post in Friends of Battle Park, the nonprofit organization raising money for the maintenance of the sacred ground under threat. The ground Pearl was protecting this morning. Ghost was past president of the group. Joansie the current president. She'd recruited Siler to stand for election as the group's next leader.

"Pour me some of that hot tea," Ghost said, his voice without the whimsy that carried his tales of R&R. He gulped from the steaming mug. His shoulders fell. His neck muscles tightened.

"Joansie and I are splitting," he said. "Nobody knows. Yet. Hold the news close for now. Marriage. Fucking marriage. I love her more than I love air. She's through with me. Done and done. Maybe I should have been better at returning calls."

Siler let out a long breath. Carla, Siler's wife, was currently on sabbatical from the marriage. She'd told him they were divorparated. At the moment, Carla was occupying their place in Valle Crucis. Siler and Carla have been married twice before. Both times to each other. Two marriages. Two divorces. Now on their third set of vows. Third strike would hurt.

"Look at us," Ghost said. "Three unwise men."

Lucinda's voice faded with the close of "Pineola." The pool players fed the juke paper money and picked their own sounds. Kate Taylor's voice shook the old speakers. *Drink a bottle full of rye.* Siler raised a glass to the pool shooters and offered to cover their next round.

My phone buzzed. Buzzed hard enough to bounce along the bar. A number my phone didn't recognize. Maybe news about Pearl. I clicked on the call. Put the phone to my ear.

"Hello," I said.

"Lassie James, please hold for Miss Emmy. The governor would like to speak with you," a man's voice said.

Chapter Three

"Hold tight," I said into the phone. "Let me get somewhere quiet."

I stepped away from the bar and walked out to the back deck. Nothing more than a landing, really. The top of the wooden staircase that served as a fire escape and an easy getaway for any customer looking to dodge friends or enemies.

The line was quiet. I stood still. No leaning against this railing.

"Hold for the governor," a man's voice said.

I counted to six before I heard the next voice.

"Lassiter James Battle," Miss Emmy said, syrup in her voice. "My honeybun. My honeybun. You are still my honeybun, aren't you?"

"Sure," I said.

"There I go, last year awarding you the bluest ribbon in my drawer, recognition from the Order of the Dogwood, for solving the murder of Dr. Mallette. Damned if you didn't send your own girlfriend to prison for the crime and marry the dead man's daughter. Called you my honeybun in front of God and country," she said. "Right there on the Capitol steps. Then hosted you at my table at Ethan's Oyster Bar. Bought you all the Cedar Island oysters you could eat."

She paused. I said nothing.

"And today my security detail interrupts me from a manicure to tell me . . . what do you guess they told me, honeybun?" Miss Emmy said. Less syrup in her voice now.

Phone stuck to my ear. She could hear me breathing. I said nothing.

"Goddammit, Lassie! You have some fucking talent for picking women," she said. "One lover in federal prison and the other in the pokey. Do you pick crazy women or do they land in your bed sane and then you fuck 'em crazy?"

"Maybe a little of both," I said.

"Well, now, honeybun. I have spent the day examining this morning's nasty cloud. I have found the lining. Let me tell you what we're gonna do," Miss Emmy said.

She talked. I listened. I assumed her staff was on the line taking notes.

Four weeks away from the gubernatorial debate and five weeks out from Election Day, Miss Emmy explained how we could help each other.

"I can't fix it for Pearl, but I can help you," she said. "Put a less generous way, I can increase your hurt. You pick."

Ultimately, she reminded me, she had the power to issue pardons. Before Pearl had to suffer a long prison sentence, Miss Emmy could pardon her. That is, if and only if Miss Emmy were re-elected. Among other things, the prospect of a pardon required my endorsement of her candidacy. Required me to join her at rallies here and there across the state. And she wanted original research.

Her interest in my endorsement caught me by surprise. She took my silence as a question.

"Yes, honeybun, in my world of Tar Heel state politics, which is really the only world that matters, you have become a bonafide celebrity," Miss Emmy said. She added extra syrup when she said the word *bonafide*. "Sitting in Pig Farm Tavern with one little laptop computer, you embarrassed the FBI and solved the most notorious murder this century. My pollsters tell me you have done the un-fucking-doable: you appeal to professoriate *and* proletariat. And along the way, your murderer girlfriend made an orphan of the woman you married. Both of 'em cover girls. If you didn't exist, honeybun, the tabloids would invent you."

I ignored the syrup.

"You mentioned research," I said. "What is it you want?"

She feared a lawsuit, she informed me. A collection of her pig farming and barbecue selling competitors was preparing to sue Miss Emmy's Barbecue Shacks for fraud. If she couldn't head off the lawsuit, she expected a public filing accusing her of adding pig from Iowa farms to the chopped pork in her signature Miss Emmy's Carolina BBQ sandwiches. A politician could withstand all kinds of charges, true or false, but hog treason would be electoral death in North Carolina.

"Every fucking speck of pig in my sandwiches comes from farms around Clinton, down in Sampson County," she said. "And I mean we run the stinkingest, loudest, pig-shittiest hog farms in the world. That's how we get the best-tasting pig meat. The seasoning differs from one end of the state to the other, I grant you. And maybe we're using electric cookers, not charring the pig over hickory fire. Tho' our cookers produce the best Grade A burnt pig flesh in the world, no matter what that sociology professor says on CNN. Point is, every bit of hog meat I sell is carved from the bones of a pig that died with snout full of North Carolina mud."

Miss Emmy's North Carolina hog competitors were lashing out at her chain, she contended, because her business was "vertically fucking integrated." Miss Emmy's hog farms send product to Miss Emmy's processing facilities, which send the final product out to her barbecue shacks via Miss Emmy's Pig Fleet, her trucking business. Her efficiencies allowed her to sell BBQ sandwiches at low prices. Prices so low her competitors couldn't match them. Thus, the revenge lawsuit. A nuisance suit, by her account. The competing farmers and sandwich sellers believed the announcement of the lawsuit would harm her business, even if the case later failed on the merits.

"I need that research magic of yours, that same magic you used to outsmart the FBI," she said. "Need you to dig up something that will keep these hog enemies from dragging me into court. Need it now, Lassie. Need it before this damned debate."

I could see Orion in the night sky. For the first time all day, I felt cold. I thought about Pearl. Imagined the chill of her concrete cell. I needed the promise of a pardon.

"Assuming I can make good on your asks," I said. "What can you do for us? What can you do beyond the pardon? I mean I don't want it to get that far. I need to head off a conviction. Let's play this out. Say I show up at your rallies and do the endorsement thing. And I figure out the research. All hoping for a pardon that may or may not arrive. For sake of conversation, let's imagine a pathway where I satisfy all of your requirements and Pearl's problems all go away."

This time the line was quiet on her end. Then, finally, "Eugenia, hang up the phone. Write up the notes and send everything to me tonight."

Click.

"R&R," she said. "R&R is on the bench tomorrow. That kind of luck comes with a price. You won't see me in the courtroom tomorrow, but you'll see my good work. You'll know I'm there, honeybun. A few people still owe Miss Emmy favors. Favors that I can steer this way or that, favors I can steer to make life good for a friend or to make life miserable for somebody else. For sake of conversation, as you say, favors come to those who do good things."

I didn't know whether to call her bluff or not. Maybe R&R was the luck of the draw, based on who'd been next in line for the court calendar. Or maybe Miss Emmy could turn dials and move levers. Maybe she could be the invisible hand that would keep Pearl from jail.

"Pearl's stunt this morning shook the campaign like a snow globe. She gave me an opening. I believe I can exploit this moment without coming off as the heavy. It's a moment when I can cut Doll off at the knees without the public seeing anything but a smile on my face," Miss Emmy said. "It's all about the R. One tiny letter, one big difference."

Had no idea what to say. Miss Emmy filled the silence.

"Difference between pretty and petty," she said. "One tiny letter. The R. We politicians can be as petty as we wanna be as long as the voters see the R. We want them to see us as pretty. Always pretty. As pretty as the Dutch Tulip lacquer on my nails."

The Hemingway line leapt into my mind. Were we Jake and Brett?

"The people of North Carolina will see the light. I'm not the Republican you want, honeybun. I'm the Republican you need. The people of North Carolina will think it so," she said. "So long as we help them get there."

I needed Miss Emmy on Pearl's side. More important, I didn't want Miss Emmy as an enemy.

"You got it, Miss Emmy. I'm in," I said.

23

"Honeybun, my honeybun, I can taste the sugar on your lips," she said as she hung up the line.

A star in Orion's Belt blinked. I saw it.

Back in Pig Farm, I briefed Siler. Ghost was gone. Siler poured from a fresh pot of genmaicha. The tea beat back the chill. Realized I'd had nothing to eat all day. I was all of a sudden hungry. Took the last sandwich from Siler's cooler.

Siler had Ella's "Lost Berlin Tapes" album playing on the juke. *Excuse me while I disappear.* Ella sang. I ate. Siler closed his eyes and floated away.

Stomach full and adrenalin spent, I used the last fuel in my tank to walk the two blocks to our home on Friendly Lane. Sanders Mallette, Pearl's father, had lived here. The professor who changed my life. The man chosen to lead the University out of a dark period. The man murdered by Dr. Holly Pike, the woman we all knew as Fats. The woman, as Miss Emmy reminded me, who had been my long-ago college girlfriend and a once-again fling. The woman who turned out to be a murderess.

Mallette's house became Pearl's house and then, once we married, our house. Now I was entering the Queen Anne alone. A place turned dark without Pearl's light. Dark walk past the honey locust trees framing the driveway. Dark entryway. Dark kitchen. Dark stairs. Dark bedroom.

I twisted the rod to open the blinds. I raised a window to bring moonlight into the bedroom. Too tired to wash my face, I fell asleep on top of the quilt. Fell asleep in my clothes, still smelling of the crushed leaves from Battle Park and the whiskey from Pig Farm. Fell asleep on my side of the bed.

I dreamed of waking up ahead of the sunrise to smells and noises from the kitchen. In my dreams, I found Pearl placing hand pies on cooling racks. Hot from the oven, sweet potato hand pies. Pearl winked at me and laughed. She knew sweet potato pies were the one dessert I didn't like. Rack after rack, she filled the grates with sweet potato pies. Her yellow hair hanging past her shoulders, dusted with flour. Sweet potato chandeliers swinging from the ceiling. Then I saw the walls smeared with whipped sweet potatoes.

I woke up. My head hurt. Whiskey had left my mouth dry. Like my teeth were wearing little angora sweaters, as Ghost used to say after a night of dorm drinking. I got up and washed my face and scrubbed my teeth with mint paste and gargled with the harshest mouthwash in the cabinet. It was after 3 a.m. Pearl's first appearance six hours away.

Back to the bed, a maple leaf had blown in the window and landed on Pearl's pillow. A leaf as dark and red as the blood Pearl drew from Stokes's nose.

I dialed Pearl's cell phone to hear her voice inviting callers to leave a message.

"Pearl here. Leave your number or send a text," her voice said. I put it on speaker and called four times.

I texted her blue hearts.

Lying there in a half-empty bed, I prayed a selfish prayer. I prayed to die before Pearl. Unmarried for a half-century and comfortable alone in the world for so long, I was now in such love with this woman that I couldn't describe a future without her. I knew she'd be fine in a world where I passed first. She was ferocious. Her passing would stop my heart. A prison sentence for her would kill me. Couldn't imagine her imprisoned for years. A selfish prayer. I was not fearful for her suffering behind bars. I was scared of how I would suffer without her hand to hold, without her biting my bottom lip when we kissed, without her forehead bumping against mine.

I prayed myself to sleep, frightened out of my mind.

25

Chapter Four

"All rise," the bailiff said. His voice bounced off the Chapel Hill courtroom's back wall.

R&R emerged from chambers. Black robe zipped to the neck, to the edge of his Carolina blue bowtie. The bailiff held R&R's arm as the old man navigated the two steps to the judicial bench. Court files and a steaming mug of coffee were already at his place.

"Good morning. Good morning," R&R said. "What an occasion to see this small corner of American government filled with fans of the criminal procedure. Ms. Tenley, is the state prepared to proceed with the calendar."

The courtroom's eight rows of pews were filled, except for spots the bailiff had reserved in the first row, squarely behind the prosecutor's table. Pearl was still in a back room, in the holding area alongside the others in pre-trial detention who had scheduled appearances today. The defendant's table, for the moment, was empty.

ADA Susannah Tenley stood to represent the state. Tenley grew up on Key Biscayne, the only child of Cuban-American parents. She moved to North Carolina to attend Duke Law School and never left. In a town of smart people, she and her wife, a commercial pilot, stood out for their brainpower.

She responded to R&R without emotion.

"The state is ready to proceed, Your Honor," she said.

The bailiff recognized Tenley's nod and opened the door to the holding room. He escorted seven defendants to the jury box. Pearl was in the group.

"We'll begin with first appearances," Tenley said. "Is counsel for Pearl Mallette here?"

All part of the ritual. Tenley had been talking with Ghost ten minutes before the judge arrived. She knew he was standing along the far wall, the gathering spot for attorneys with items on the morning calendar.

Ghost took his spot at the defense table. The bailiff brought Pearl over to take the chair beside him. He placed a satchel by her chair. From it, Pearl retrieved a brush and ran it through her hair. Once groomed, with her free hand she pulled the loose hairs from the brush then realized she didn't have any place to drop the strands. She gripped them in her left hand. Absent the jacket, she was wearing the outfit from the Battle Park appearance the morning prior.

"Good morning, Judge. Argus Peppers here. This is my client, Pearl Mallette," Ghost said.

In a clean suit and pressed shirt, Ghost was rumpled.

"Your Honor," Tenley said, taking the script, "Ms. Mallette faces a number of charges related to an incident in Battle Park yesterday morning. The state is prepared to review the charges at this time."

Both Ghost and Tenley were standing.

"Hold steady, Ms. Tenley. Hold on," R&R said. He removed his glasses with his left hand and wiped his eyes with this right.

Tenley took her seat first, clearly aware of the theater at hand. Ghost followed. He had a fountain pen resting cross-wise on a leather folio on the table. He opened the folio and flipped the legal pad to a blank page and removed the top from the pen, the kind of writing instrument I saw Tories using when I ran the London bureau for *The Post*. Blue marbled casing, gold trim. A Conway Stewart pen, best I could recall. Ghost was ready to commit to paper whatever came next from R&R. Tenley had a wilted accordion file container in front of her, its sagging corner matched to the corner of the table. No pen, no paper in front of Tenley. She had three red rubber bands around her left wrist, precious government-issue office supplies.

R&R prolonged the eye-wiping bit. As much auteur as judge, R&R sped up or slowed down the judicial business as he wanted. Just then, I saw Corn Stalks come down the middle aisle and take the open spots in the pew behind Tenley. The encounter with the bitternut left shades of blue across Stokes's face. Black jeans, burgundy mock turtleneck. He yelped when he sat down, the result of Pearl's busting up his ribs. Cornelia showed me her middle finger after assisting Stokes into the pew. She was in the same puffy pirate shirt, or a clone, and red Levi's. THAI scarf around her neck.

R&R's slow walk-up to Pearl's first appearance bought time for Corn Stalks to join the show. Their presence was unrelated and unnecessary to the minimal proceedings of a routine first appearance. Maybe Miss Emmy was right. Maybe R&R's orchestrations revealed her presence.

"Lots of interesting characters in my courtroom, today," R&R said. "I'd like to get to know everybody a bit, have a nice chat."

Tenley sat straight as a spindle. Ghost replaced the Conway Stewart pen cap then removed it again.

"Madame Assistant District Attorney, good morning, again," R&R said.

"You and I are old friends. Everyone here probably assumes that. I want to affirm it here. I see it's a three-rubber band morning for you. I trust you and your bride are well? How's life on that dairy farm of yours?"

"Peachy, your honor," Tenley said, standing again. "Ann is in the air this morning. Cows are on the ground. Milk is flowing like, well, milk."

"Perhaps you two might add honeybees to that land of milk," R&R said.

Tenley nodded. Took her seat. R&R turned his shoulders a few degrees to square up with the defense table.

"Mr. Peppers, life as a barrister fits you well," R&R said. "Tell me about that pen."

Court watchers leaned in various directions to gain a view. Ghost explained the pen was a gift from Siler, who acquired it as part of a blind purchase of an orphaned storage locker.

"Conway Stewart, circa 1955," Ghost said, "plus or minus."

"Oh, you're not under oath," R&R said, drawing laughter from court watchers. "Enjoy that pen, young man. Makes me wonder what measure you will take to return the favor to Mr. Siler."

Ghost nodded. Less said the better at such a moment. I couldn't tell where R&R was taking this. It was something less than testimony, more than conversation.

"Miss Pearl. Miss Pearl, Miss Pearl," R&R said. "I admired your daddy more than I admired anyone on the campus across the street here. I can't imagine the pain of losing him the way you did. The way we all did. I am sorry this is the occasion that provides me a chance to share my words. It reflects my failure to reach out to you last year. Please forgive me, Miss Pearl."

Pearl looked at her attorney. Ghost nodded and mouthed "thank you" to Pearl.

"Thank you," she said. Ghost nodded at her again.

"Your Honor," Pearl added. With another nudge from Ghost, she stood up. "Thank you, Your Honor. I recall my dad's stories about visiting with you on your porch. Those evenings when you hosted pickers."

Ghost touched Pearl's arm to indicate she'd done enough free-lancing. She sat.

"Oh, my," R&R said. "The sounds of the mandolins and banjos. And your daddy loved the psaltery. Your recollection reminds me to invite those pickers back to my porch. I will be sure you receive an invitation."

R&R scribbled a note on a pad.

"Miss Pearl," R&R said, leading forward and adding more bass to his voice. "Are you today's hero or villain?"

"Your Honor!" Shrieks in stereo. Ghost and Tenley both on their feet.

R&R laughed. Pearl, cool in the moment, retrieved the brush from the satchel and ran the brush through her hair with exaggerated strokes. She shook her hair back and forth and sat up tall and let the hair from her left-hand drop to the floor. Her shoulders straight and high. Her body said what her attorney didn't want her to utter.

"Be seated, counselors, crisis averted," R&R said. "Miss Pearl, the lawyers are correct. You needn't speak—yet. Instead, I want you to be thinking about what you'll say in a few minutes when I circle back to you. The state is going to want to keep you right where you are. Mr. Peppers is going to argue for your release, on the promise you will be in court at the appointed date and time. Be thinking about what you will say when I ask you whether we can trust you to do this. Whether we can trust you to refrain from picking up guns and knives and things. Whether we can trust you to let Mr. Avery and Miss Sloop be."

Ghost put his hand over Pearl's mouth.

"Right, right, right," R&R said. "Not now, Miss Pearl. I'll come back to you. Keep thinking. Your brain is shiny and alive, I know. You will find answers in it."

"Your Honor. The people are prepared to move forward with today's calendar, starting with Ms. Mallette's first appearance," Tenley said, standing again.

"Yes, yes, yes," R&R said. "This rush to go, go, go. It reminds me how sweet the tobacco would get when we'd let it cure in those barns, wrapped in fire and smoke. I tended those fires, Madame Assistant District Attorney, in my youth. Stayed there overnight. All night, every night. Through many summer weeks. Watching that smoke dance through the flue to the sky. As long as I did absolutely nothing, the smoke from those fires made a leaf that tasted better on the lips than any leaf in the world. I find myself wishing more people would do less of whatever it is they are doing these days. Sometimes the world is sweeter when we do less. Don't you think, Miss Tenley?"

The ADA took her seat. I could hear Miss Emmy's voice in R&R's. Miss Emmy knew there would be no court reporter covering routine proceedings in District Court. A judge could turn a first appearance into most any kind of thing he wanted. Or anything she wanted.

"Now, Mr. Avery? Mr. Avery, are you with us today?" R&R said, looking over his glasses in a pretend search for the man he knew to be a few feet behind Tenley. "Please stand and be recognized if you are with us today."

Cornelia held his arm. She helped Stokes to his feet.

"Good morning, Mr. Avery," R&R said. "What a luxury to have an attractive woman as your aide. I spent much of the middle half-century of my life trying to figure out how to appear helpless in such a way as to attract a nightingale. On another day, I wish for you to tell me your secret. All the men here are envious of your success. All of us who stand and sit without the feminine strength to which you subscribe."

Tenley's shoulders sagged an inch.

Stokes looked to his right and left and to the back of Tenley's head. Anticipating no role in the first appearance proceeding, he had no legal representation. The silence seemed to heighten his pain. He reached out and rested his right arm on Cornelia's shoulder.

"Yes, Your Honor. I am lucky to have Cornelia," he said.

"I am sorry not to have met you before today," R&R said. "By way of confession, I was not aware of you before yesterday. Then around noon, at just the moment when the waitress at Sutton's served me two hot dogs, a second waitress ran to us. She asked me to watch something on her phone. What I saw gave the appearance of a moving picture. It started with you by a tree at Battle Park. It ended with you on the ground at Battle Park. The cinematography, I want to note, was below what even an old man from Goldsboro would expect. More Fellini than Capra, if you ask me. Tell me, Mr. Avery, what brought you to Battle Park yesterday?"

"Your Honor!" Shrieks in stereo again. Tenley and Ghost firing objections at the judge.

"The state would ask the court to agree that this is not the time or the place to establish a legal foundation for the facts of this case," Tenley said, her voice loud enough to hush up Ghost. "And the state is not going to litigate the merits today. We are here for Ms. Mallette's first appearance and then will move on, and move with some speed, to the many other items on today's calendar."

To provide an explanation point, Tenley poked the table with her pointer finger.

"One hundred percent, Madame Assistant District Attorney," R&R said. "I agree. We are doing none of those things today. What this is, what I encourage everyone here to appreciate, is more modest. It is a conversation. I like to get to know visitors here in my courtroom. Spring of next year will bring my 90th birthday. I see it on the horizon, the ninth of ten markers toward my century. In these decades, I have come to appreciate conversation. One person says something to another person, who listens and reflects and responds. Back and forth. For those unfamiliar with the art, this morning may be revelatory. For me, my aspiration is beneath anything close to a revelation. A conversation, nothing more."

Tenley was back in her chair. Shoulders slumping another inch. Ghost had the cap off his pen.

"Again, Mr. Avery, what brought you to Battle Park yesterday? Is this a regular spot for your morning hikes?" R&R asked.

"Business, Your Honor," Stokes said. "Business."

"Do tell," R&R said. "Business fascinates me nearly as much as flue-cured tobacco."

Chapter Five

Nowhere to hide, Stokes proceeded to describe how he and Cornelia had co-founded the business, Corn Stalks. Working out of Sanford, they designed and built commercial and residential real estate projects in North Carolina and South Carolina. For some time, he said, Corn Stalks had been in negotiations with the University of North Carolina to purchase large parcels of land that a donor had gifted to the University as part of settling an estate.

In recent months, a deal had come together. Corn Stalks would purchase 2,000 acres in Caldwell County, in North Carolina's western Piedmont, and about 100,000 acres in Park and Sweet Grass counties, in Montana. This would create a cash windfall for the University and put idle land back into use, generating jobs and local property taxes. A win-win for the communities and for the University, according to Stokes.

Stokes paused to shift his weight. Cornelia squeezed his hand.

"Battle Park?" R&R asked.

Stokes let out a breath. As he worked with university officials to reach terms on the North Carolina and Montana land deals, he explained, he approached his investors about the idea of adding Battle Park to the mix. Corn Stalks understood any purchase of such prized land would require a premium price. His investors stepped up and offered partnership terms that worked for everyone. With the forthcoming vote, the university trustees would approve the deal.

"And that's how we get to the billion-dollar price tag I'm reading about," R&R said. "A package deal."

"More or less, yes, Your Honor," Stokes said.

"Sounds like more to me," R&R said.

He asked if Cornelia had any corrections or amendments to offer. She declined. She remained seated. Stokes remained standing.

"Mr. Avery," R&R said. "Do you know what Paul said to the Corinthians about this kind of deal?"

"No, Your Honor. I don't," Stokes said.

"I didn't think so," R&R said.

The judge's expression held steady. Court watchers laughed.

"Fortune smiles on you and your bride," R&R said. "Imagine the luck of having this kind of vote come before a governing board of which you and your bride are members."

Cornelia squeezed her husband's hand again. R&R ignored Pearl's hoot. Ghost put down his pen and touched her arm. R&R waved Tenley off when she stood to speak.

"Mr. Avery, what plans do you have for Battle Park? Trail maintenance, perhaps?" R&R said.

"Yes to trail improvements," Stokes said. "Lots of improvements in store."

Stokes took the bait. Thank you, Miss Emmy.

Stokes raised his voice: "The 93 acres have been just sitting there, no one lifting a finger to improve them. Hard as that is to believe. Place is a mess. Covered in dirt and mud. Filled with bugs and weeds. Chaos, really. Not a decent flower bed or garden row in the whole place. No benches! Or nearly none. And the one we sat on ruined Cornelia's white Levi's. How can they even call it a park when there are no rides, no snack bar, no water fountains?"

A half-dozen court watchers wearing THAI scarves applauded. Tenley stood up to speak. R&R again waved her off. He ignored the applause. He gave Stokes more rope. Stokes told the judge how The Cabins at Battle Park would bring 15 authentic log homes to the woods.

"Mansions, really," Stokes said, "not the kind of log cabins you're thinking of."

"Even an old man from Goldsboro understands we find all types of log cabins in the world, Mr. Avery," R&R said.

Stokes kept at it: "We are importing this amazing wood from Finland. The Finns really know how to build a cabin. And saunas. Kontio Arctic Pine. Yeah, that's it. We'll have the 15 homes, all with saunas, made from this Finland tree wood, and the lodge with 15 suites."

"Not a tree in North Carolina will suit?" R&R said, egging on Stokes.

"No, no. No loblolly in our mansions. This Finland tree wood is amazing," Stokes said. "And, Judge, do you know how the old moonshiners would hide their stills in hollers and in underground bunkers?"

"Tell me more," R&R said, failing to mention how Daddy Roberts had run his own still in Wayne County's Buck Swamp.

"We'll hollow out a hillside and build the Battle Branch Distillery," Stokes said. "It will be sort of underneath and alongside the old Forest Theatre. The entrance will be at the Sourwood Loop trail head, right there at the curve in the road. We'll fix up the hillside beside Forest Theatre real nice.

We have some amazing landscaping in mind. Turn this place into a real park. Make it worthy of being called a park."

"What a gift," R&R said.

"I'll be sure you get the first bottle of whiskey from the distillery," Stokes said. He was talking with his hands now. Full of himself. Benefitting from some kind of adrenaline emitted from the real estate developer gland.

"I will leave a light on for you, Mr. Avery," R&R said.

I thought for a second the judge was going to call him honeybun.

R&R again asked Cornelia if she had anything to add. She stood up and talked about her work as a landscape design architect. She talked about her vision for improving upon Battle Park's untended scrabble. Not an ounce of order to it, she proclaimed. Bragging about her recent work, Cornelia directed the judge to take note of the treescape along the Interstate 85 exit to Fair Play, South Carolina.

"Exit 4," Stokes said. "The folks at Exit 4 love Cornelia."

"I do know a reliable hot dog stand there on Old Dobbins Bridge Road," R&R said. "Gibson's, I believe it is. Those hot dogs were the best part of our family vacations on Tugaloo Bay. You tell Mr. Gibson when you see him that I'll be back there soon enough and want to see Miss Cornelia's fine trees. After the hot dogs, of course."

The half-dozen fans in THAI scarves applauded again. Cornelia turned and curtsied, her hands holding the hem of an imaginary skirt. Stokes waved. They both sat down.

R&R handed his coffee mug to the bailiff and asked for a refill.

"All this talk of Gibson's has me wishing we were at lunch break. Cyril, while you're getting the coffee, please call Sutton's and put in my order," he said.

Ghost had written down everything Stokes and Cornelia said. He'd set aside his pen and was stretching his hand.

"Mr. Battle? Lassiter James Battle. I believe that is the correct name for you, sir?" R&R was looking right at me. I stood.

"Yes, sir," I said, then corrected myself. "Yes, Your Honor."

"A fast edit there," R&R said. "A skill sharpened in newsrooms? I remember reading tales of your work to solve the murder of Miss Pearl's Daddy. Your intimacy in that case was unusual, if I recall correctly. With the accused, in fact. What occupies your time these days?"

I recited the headlines from my CV. Journalism professor, recently appointed. Fellow at the Mallette Center for Public Service. Returned to Chapel Hill for my Ph.D. after working as a journalist in London, Washington, D.C., Winston-Salem and a few other spots.

"And a man with gifts of persuasion," R&R said.

"Excuse me, Your Honor?" I said.

"There was a time when Miss Pearl was not your wife. Today she is. I can only conclude that this transformation occurred because you are a world-class persuader," R&R said.

"You are generous, Your Honor," I said. Happy to play along. I could hear Miss Emmy now, for sure.

"Mr. Peppers was bragging about you to me early this morning before the bailiff brought us to order. Mr. Peppers tells me you are a song-writer," R&R said.

Tenley was leaning forward now, face in her hands. Her back round, shoulders soft. R&R ignored another hoot from Pearl.

"Ghost is also generous, far too generous," I said. "Mr. Peppers, that is."

"On that future day when Miss Pearl visits my porch to hear the pickers, we will enjoy a song of yours," R&R said. "May your fame grow to match that of Miss Cornelia's at Exit 4."

From the corner of my eye, I saw Joansie slide into the courtroom through a side door. She stood in the line of attorneys along the far wall. Attorneys on hand to handle their calendar items now had front-row seats for R&R's show.

R&R cleared his throat. Took two swallows of coffee from the newly filled mug. The all-business tone was back in his voice as he reviewed the charges with Pearl. The two misdemeanors and the felony. Pearl nodded that she understood them. Then she said "yes" out loud, when R&R required a verbal answer. In response to R&R's invitation for the state to add or change any charges, Tenley declined.

More theater. The state could bring any charges to the grand jury and secure an indictment. If the DA's office opted to do that quickly, there would be no need for a probable cause hearing. The DA's office held all the options. It could delay its presentation to the grand jury and use the probable cause hearing to pressure-test its case. Then even if the judge ruled against the state at probable cause, then the DA could always still go to the grand jury. With politically sticky cases, the DA could let the probable cause hearing decision stand. If the state prevailed at the hearing, the case would be bound over for trial in Superior Court. With a loss at the probable cause hearing, the DA could use that decision as an exit ramp. Wash its hands of a loser of a case.

"Madame Assistant District Attorney and Mr. Peppers, I want to handle two pieces of business here before Cyril signals that my hot dogs have arrived. One, let's set a date for the probable cause hearing. The other is to reach a decision on where Miss Pearl will spend her time between now and the hearing."

"Your Honor," Tenley said, jumping in, "the state would like to schedule this before the end of the year. I am looking at December dates now. I have January dates, also, if that timing works better for Your Honor."

"Next week," Ghost said, sending a buzz through court watchers. "Monday works for us."

"Your Honor," Tenley said, "the state objects."

R&R flipped through pages as if to consult his calendar.

"How about Tuesday?" he said. "That day is free on my calendar."

"We will be here Tuesday, Your Honor," Ghost said, before Tenley could speak.

R&R nodded to Tenley.

"Miss Tenley, the District Attorney's Office is filled with smart legal minds. I am certain one of them can manage a probable cause hearing on Tuesday," R&R said.

"And the state objects to bail," Tenley said, hoping to balance out the scheduling loss with a win on custody.

"Your Honor, I'd like to be heard," Ghost said. He was on his feet.

"No, no. I'll be heard now," R&R said.

Ghost sat down.

"Miss Pearl, I kept my promise to you and gave you time to think about those questions I mentioned before, back before the talk of hot dogs and Miss Cornelia's artistry at Exit 4," R&R said. "I'm ready to hear from you now. First off, how do you feel about scheduling your probable cause hearing for Tuesday. Right here, in front of me. Cyril will be here, too. Mr. Peppers can be here. And the district attorney will find someone to be here. How do you feel?"

Pearl looked at Ghost. He nodded to her. Nudged her arm to remind her to stand. She spoke and affirmed the decision for the Tuesday hearing.

"Now about your freedom," R&R said. "People do funny things with freedom. Sometimes they drive carpool. Sometimes they shoot guns. Sometimes they disappear. What about you, Miss Pearl? Do you have a passport?"

"Expired," she said. "I have a passport. It is expired, Your Honor."

"Are you expecting the United States government to deliver a new one to you before Tuesday? Have you submitted an application for a new passport?" R&R said.

Pearl shook her head and then verbalized the answer. No passport application under review.

"What is your professional line of work, Miss Pearl? Or do you have one? I should start there," R&R said.

Pearl explained that she works as a genealogist. She conducted research and produced reports for clients who hired her. Recent clients had included individuals, lawyers and producers from TV shows that reveal family histories. Replying to R&R's questions, Pearl confirmed that her work had often required travel. Before the judge could ask, she said that after losing her dad she had slowed down her professional research. She had no current plans for or need for travel.

"If the state keeps you in this jail, I know you will be here next week," R&R said. "If I let you out of the jail, what will you do? What will come of you?"

"I will be here, Your Honor," Pearl said. Responding to Ghost's nudge, she continued, "I will be here. I will stay out of trouble. I will, uh. I will. I mean, you will not regret your decision to let me leave the jail."

R&R smiled.

"Regret prevention insurance," R&R said. "Wise. Wise woman. I was right about your shiny brain. While we're moving at double time, let's check off the arraignment box, also. Do you have a plea in mind, Miss Pearl?"

"Not guilty, Your Honor," Ghost said. "My client pleads not guilty."

R&R secured the necessary affirmation from Pearl. He then turned back toward the court watchers and looked at me.

"Mr. Battle," he said, "are you any relation to Kemp Plumber Battle? Any relation to the man, to the family for whom the park is named?"

"No, Your Honor," I said. "Pearl and I have tried to find a connection. Lots of research. No connection that we can find."

"Mr. Battle, you are aware that if your wife absconds, that if you assist her in absconding, or if for any reason other than her death she does not appear in front of me on time next week, you are aware, Mr. Battle, that marshals will tear down your house and bury you on my farm. Bury you alive. With isopropyl alcohol poured onto the scratches you will suffer from the feral cats that live in my woods. You are aware, are you not?" R&R said.

"I am aware, Your Honor."

R&R looked at Tenley and back at Ghost. Pearl followed the wave of his hand and took her seat again.

"I will write up an order releasing Miss Pearl immediately from jail. It will require her to wear an ankle bracelet and require her to remain within a 500-foot radius of the house on . . ."

R&R looked at me, then at Pearl.

"Friendly Lane," we said at the same time.

"She must stay within a 500-foot radius of the house on Friendly Lane. If the ankle bracelet alarm sounds, I will have deputies return Miss Pearl to the county jail."

Before Ghost could stop her, Pearl was on her feet.

"Your Honor, may I be heard? Is that the way to say it?" Pearl said.

R&R looked at Cyril and raised his eyebrows. "Hot dogs not here yet," the bailiff said.

"Miss Pearl, are you about to negotiate with me?" R&R said.

"How would the court feel about a range of 8,000 feet to the east of Friendly Lane and 4,000 feet to the south?" Pearl said.

Tenley rubbed her eyes. Ghost got his pen ready to write.

"Miss Pearl, the specificity of your request reminds me of the precision my daddy used when lying to my mama and, all the while, sounding honest as Lincoln," R&R said. "Please explain."

Pearl took a breath and spoke. Sunrise Biscuit Kitchen was a short drive to the east, about 8,000 feet, by her quick calculation. The grave of her father, in the old cemetery on campus, was about 4,000 feet south of home. She cautioned that the distances would need to be confirmed. Pearl offered her attorney's services for the task. Ghost stopped writing.

"How often do you visit your daddy's resting place?" R&R asked.

"Every morning," Pearl said. R&R turned and looked at me. I nodded.

R&R turned back to Pearl.

"Well, how often do you go to Sunrise Biscuit Kitchen?" R&R asked.

"Every morning," Pearl said, "Every morning after my walk to Dad's grave."

R&R looked in my direction again. I nodded.

Cyril cleared his throat and tilted his head toward the judge's chambers.

"It is time for hot dogs," R&R said. "Miss Pearl, the order will permit you the distance from your doorway on Friendly Lane to your daddy's resting place. The order will require Mr. Peppers or his designee to bring you the biscuits. I will see you Tuesday morning."

"All rise!" Cyril shouted.

R&R was gone, into chambers for his Sutton's lunch.

Then I saw Siler for the first time. Standing along the back wall of the courtroom. He held a coffee cup in his left hand. He was working his phone with his right.

Pearl ran through the swinging gate separating the pews from the judicial business. We met in the center aisle. She hugged me. She kissed me. She pressed her forehead against mine. I closed my eyes and saw Tuna Canyon. To my right, the sun was dropping behind the outline of a crooked rock. To my left, pink and orange sunset dripped onto the Pacific blue and white. I could see Pearl dancing in dusk's fading light. She wore the straw hat her dad kept on the hook beside the back door at their house in Maine. She was curling a finger, pulling me in her direction, pulling me toward her dance.

She kissed me again right there in the courtroom, and the daydream burst was over.

She leaned forward to whisper in my ear.

"You heard the judge. You're the designee. Go get me a fucking biscuit. Ghost will take me home to greet the ankle bracelet," Pearl said.

She bit my lip. She turned and disappeared.

Chapter Six

FRIDAY MORNING, OCTOBER 4TH

The butterscotch leather seats in the Bombardier 6000 jet were soft as cake icing. I thought about licking the headrest. Instead, I drank from the mug of steaming genmaicha the steward delivered on a tray.

We'd taken a daybreak flight with Miss Emmy to the North Carolina mountains. After rallies in West Jefferson and Sugar Grove, her driver steered the SUV down Candy Lane to Bamboo Road and onto the apron where the private jet was waiting to lift us into the sky above Boone.

Wheels up, the window view of crimson and pumpkin-colored foliage calmed my mind. Buzz of my phone startled me. Text from Pearl. Ghost was late with what she called her "court-ordered biscuit." I searched for a where-the-fuck-is-my-biscuit emoji to send Ghost. Then I remembered he didn't keep his phone handy. Texted Pearl a blue heart emoji and assurances that her attorney would appear.

Today was my day to make good on the promise to join Miss Emmy on the stump. At the morning rallies, a youth quartet from Fig, a mountain village by the North Fork New River, joined Miss Emmy to perform "Keep on the Sunny Side" and "Will the Circle Be Unbroken."

Now Miss Emmy had Carter Family tunes running through the airplane's sound system. *It'll aggravate your soul . . .*

"In the histories of recorded music and powered flight, I do believe this is the first instance when A.P. Carter accompanied a luxury jet headed to Conetoe, North Carolina," Siler said.

"Greenville, Siler," Miss Emmy said. "We're flying into the heart of Pitt County. Used to be the largest producer of flue-cured tobacco in the world. Now a medical school sits on those old cigarette fields."

Siler nodded and put buds in his ears. Selected music from his phone.

After rallies in Greenville, Conetoe and Farmville, we'd fly to Chapel Hill for a late meeting in the private home of a Hillsborough donor. A nightcap, Miss Emmy called it.

"Hillsborough is Janie's people. Educated, quadratic folk," Miss Emmy said. "Conetoe and everyplace near there is all yard signs for Doll. This three-way race changes up my vote counting. Used to be, anyone not voting for me counted as a vote against me. Not anymore. Now a vote against me might go to Doll, might go to Janie."

She'd left most of her lipstick on the lip of a coffee mug. She pulled out a mirror the size of a pepperoni and re-applied paint. A victory smack signaled self-approval. Lips and fingernails once again the same shade of red.

Janie Spearman, the Democratic nominee for governor, was running strong among teachers, public employees and university types. Miss Emmy praised Janie's leadership as the state's public education chief. "I wish I could keep her in that role through my second term," Miss Emmy said. "She's a wonderful leader and a wonderful woman."

"But . . .?" I said.

"But she's not crazy enough or mean enough to be governor," Miss Emmy said.

Doll was running strong in the places where populists and know-nothings flourished. Most of her campaign involved sinking fangs in people born outside the United States. She also promoted radical, nonsensical ideas she claimed would reduce crime and save money. She promised to pardon every inmate in the state prison system, other than those on death row, on the condition that those pardoned sign a contract promising to leave the state of North Carolina. More than 30,000 inmates. Doll pledged to have busses running from the prisons to the Virginia, Tennessee and South Carolina borders and to seaports. Anyplace where her pardoned thousands could leave the state. Doll promised that closing prisons would save billions of dollars. She promised that exiling cons would lower crime rates. Doll floated the idea of establishing a border security force to protect the state's boundaries.

"And Doll is too crazy and too mean to be governor," Miss Emmy said.

"Goldilocks theory," I said.

"Yep," Miss Emmy said. "I'm just right. I'm just the right amount of crazy and mean to serve the people of North Carolina."

I smiled.

"Means a lot to have you with me today, honeybun," Miss Emmy said. "It's a chance to invite some new folks onto our bandwagon."

I had been dreading this. As it turned out, the morning rallies were fine. Miss Emmy didn't attempt to script me. Told me to talk about whatever I wanted, whatever was in my heart. I talked for a few minutes about the awe-inspiring natural surroundings and the wonder of the arts, pointing to the Fig quartet as a practical example. Talked about how much the children of North Carolina would benefit from spending more time in nature and more time engaged in the arts. Miss Emmy made this easy work.

"As long as your campaign can afford this jet, I'm happy to talk with folks about connecting kids to Mother Nature and the arts," I said.

"There are all kinds of donors, honeybun. Some donate cash. Some donate jets. Best I can tell, the donors sending me money are motivated by their love of North Carolina," she said.

She saw the disbelief on my face.

"Well, honeybun, yes, there are ignoble fuck-ups who attempt to sneak foreign money into campaign contributions as part of their lobbying scams," she said. "Every barrel has its bottom."

Miss Emmy let out her breath, her body sagging with the admission of dark money in her professional world. She turned her face to the airplane window and held her eyes there. When clouds obscured the view of fall color, she sat up taller and turned back to me.

"Having you here is what matters today," she said, tension returning to muscles in her shoulders.

I tilted my head toward Siler and raised my eyebrows. He was drinking coffee and listening to music on his earbuds.

"Oh," Miss Emmy said, "I invited Siler to tag along after seeing how well he's polling. Folks love him."

Siler saw us both looking in his direction and removed the earbuds to hear what we were saying.

"You're testing Siler's approval rating? Really? C'mon," I said. "Tell me the sitting governor of North Carolina is tending to substance."

Siler kept the dumb look on his face and took a big swallow of coffee. He clicked off the music from his phone. His earbuds stopped humming.

"Bootleg album of Pooky Lynne," he said. "Live show at The Cave."

"Of course, of course," Miss Emmy said as an answer to my question. "We test everything. Your approval rating is good, honeybun. Siler's is through the roof."

I pointed out to Miss Emmy that she didn't even have Siler speak at the morning rallies. She introduced him and talked about how much she loved visiting Pig Farm. Had him wave to the crowds. I didn't mention that she'd never been inside Pig Farm.

"That's the secret to his popularity," she said. "People love the silent heroes. That adventure last year solving Dr. Mallette's murder and your . . . your entanglement with that woman, Dr. Pike—the one you call Fats, right? Well, all that brought you and Siler and Pig Farm to some fame. One wave from dear Siler is worth a million dollars in TV ads. You had to notice all the Pig Farm beanies in the crowd this morning."

Siler said nothing. Put the buds back in his ears. Re-started the Pooky Lynne tunes.

Miss Emmy leaned toward me and said sotto voce, "It's what that old man on the Heartless podcast says about movie stars. Siler has it, that sexy indifference."

The buzz from my phone bailed me out. Text from Pearl. Ghost had arrived. Before I could reply, Miss Emmy was leaning in with a question.

"Hey," Miss Emmy said, again with a low voice. "Talking to Siler earlier. Do you really have a song about biscuits? I'm thinking we can add that to the rallies."

Chapter Seven

Siler and I found privacy in the big SUV parked on the edge of the Conetoe farmhouse.

The truck's windows held so much tint and smoke, no one could see in.

Miss Emmy was inside the family residence at Woodlief Farms for a private conversation with a few big donors from eastern North Carolina. The kind of donors who donate planes. The kind of donors who buy time with the governor to set forth their terms, not to listen. Donors not interested in show business, not interested in listening to the quartet from Fig or in hearing from me or from the man melting voters with sexy indifference.

The Woodlief Farms operation stretched farther than we could see. Cotton, timber and more. The stage was set up in a camera-friendly meadow, the kind of space people who've never worked on a farm like to see in movies about farms. Working farms are filled with mud and manure and machines that chew fingers. TV farms feature meadows and dells and brooks that babble. Our stage was outfitted with imported hay bales, pumpkins painted orange and gourds from faraway lands. In place of the Fig quartet, there was a church choir. We could see singers filing out of the bus. Whipping wind turned the robes into sails.

"Good weather for a Pig Farm beanie," Siler said.

In the quiet of the ride from Greenville to Conetoe, I thought about H.F.'s passing and his request. I'd reacted negatively the other night when Ghost informed me of H.F.'s wish for me to produce a memorial service for him featuring the songs from our old band's Springfest set.

"I gotta figure out this H.F. thing," I said. "If Mallette had described a last wish, or if Mom and Dad had asked for some kind of service, I'd want to get it done. I'd want somebody to tend to my wishes."

"Ghost have anything new to say on it?" Siler said.

I covered what we heard from Ghost the other night and added in detail I'd picked up since. H.F.'s request for a memorial service in Forest Theatre. That the service should include songs from Snow Camp's setlist at a Springfest concert from the previous century. Would have been April 1982. On the lawn in front of Connor Dorm. Otherwise, H.F. requested that the catering feature a seasonal menu and that spoken remarks last no longer than Lincoln's second inaugural. Which I learned was about 700 words. Point being that the Snow Camp setlist would be the star of the show.

"Persimmons?" Siler said.

"What about 'em?"

"Persimmon pudding. I'm thinking that might work for a seasonal dessert feature. Persimmons are fun. A menu of pumpkin and squash is offensive," Siler said.

"Whatever," I said. "What do you remember about the Snow Camp songs? I mean, besides the song about a biscuit. And mind you, that's not a lot to go on."

"Maybe a pear galette. A beet tapenade could work. I've got a beet guy."

"You're killing me. The catering is not my problem," I said.

"Delaney-Quinn. Have you called her?" Siler said.

Hard to believe. I'd missed the obvious. Call on H.F.'s old bandmate, Delaney-Quinn. So distracted by Pearl's arrest and her hearing, managing the grief of losing Mom and Dad, navigating this bizarre gig with Miss Emmy, I couldn't pull my mind together on this assignment from H.F. I checked my phone to see if I had her number. Before I could search for her name, the battery died. There was a tap on the window. A showrunner.

Siler cracked open the door.

"It's time," said a guy in a headset.

The cold wind grabbed us as we stepped out of the SUV. Across the meadow, voters hired to fill the space in front of the stage were moving in a line through security screenings. Miss Emmy's staff members handed every entrant a Pig Farm beanie. On our side of the meadow, Miss Emmy was wrapping up her private meeting. She had moved to the end of the porch of the big house, by the swing suspended by chain link from the porch ceiling. The money men wore tailored dark suits. She had received their direction. Guidance dispensed, the money men walked to the SUVs and departed, driving away from the candidate and her political theater. One of the dark suits approached Miss Emmy at the far end of the porch. I couldn't hear what he said. I saw her reach out with her right hand and flatten the lapel of his suit jacket and put her hand where she could feel his heartbeat through the tailored wool. After a moment, she shook her head. He turned and followed the same route as the other men in dark suits. Miss Emmy shivered. The TV cameras were aimed at the stage, away from the escaping money men.

"You know, cider would be nice for the memorial," Siler said as we walked to the stage.

The choir sang to warm up the crowd. The choir sang the hymns I recalled from the church Sundays of my youth. Hymns I grew to hate, hymns that gave me claustrophobia. All these years later, I reflected on that judgment. I was right the first time. What lousy music, these hymns. In my mind, I put on John Prine tunes. I smiled to myself as Prine sang about the level-headed dancer doing the hoochie-coo.

After more hymns, an Edgecombe County farmer introduced a Cone-toe preacher who said a prayer that included a challenge for God to boost fortunes of a high school football squad. The preacher intro-duced the Conetoe mayor, who introduced Miss Emmy who, heaven help us, introduced Siler. He waved. The beanie-covered actors hired to portray voters went nuts.

My remarks were unremarkable. Prine was playing in my head. I heard him singing about Muhlenberg County while I was talking about Edgecombe County. As I spoke, I wondered if Miss Emmy had to bus in voters from out of town because some local Peabody had already hauled paradise away from this place and from other rural towns in North Carolina. I could see that, like the first bite of cake, the morning rally in Boone would turn out to be my best one. Miss Emmy was wired to treat every rally as her first bite. Every rally was her best rally. She delivered her stump speech with enthusiasm uncommon to a scripted recitation. Maybe that's what it means to be crazy enough to be gov-ernor. Maybe it's being crazy enough to forget everything in your past and to forgo all future dreams and to believe this moment, this town, this rally, is the only moment that matters. She sure made great TV spots out of it.

I daydreamed through the rest of the rally, daydreamed about Pearl with her head on my shoulder as we floated past the ancient cypress trees on the Black River. Daydreamed about sipping whiskey at Water Grill and asking the waiter to bring us a dozen honeymoon oysters. Daydreamed about sitting with Pearl's dad on his porch, cranking the handle on the old freezer that would produce for us peach ice cream. Daydreamed through the final offerings from the choir and the photo op that had Miss Emmy pretending to be overwhelmed by the crush of the actors crowded into her path as she walked from the stage to the SUV. In the TV ad, she would look like Bobby Kennedy. Siler and I looped around the crowd and arrived at the truck ahead of her.

"What kind of song do you think John Prine would write about sexy indifference?" I said.

"Tell you what I think," Siler said. "I think sexy indifference is finished flying commercial."

Our driver stepped in ahead of Miss Emmy and started the engine.

"Honeybun, you were amazing. Thank you," Miss Emmy said as she settled into her seat and clicked the safety belt "What a show. Siler, I've never seen anyone electrify a crowd the way you do. Onward, men. Onward."

It was rinse and repeat in Greenville and Farmville. Then back to the Bombardier for takeoff and the flight plan to Chapel Hill. With every stop, Miss Emmy's energy grew. Every rally was more fuel for her. Every rally the first one for her, every rally the best-tasting one. My tank was on empty. Siler seemed immune to it all. Energy level even-steven the whole day.

Back in the butterscotch seats on the Bombardier, I had the steward find me a power cord for my phone. He brought a glass of Bulleit Rye with ice without me asking. I kept reminding myself I was doing this for Pearl.

To buy pardon insurance. I closed my eyes as I repeated this to myself, a mantra. I needed it to get through the nightcap in Hillsborough.

I opened my eyes and sipped the rye. The sugar and alcohol soaked into the wiring behind my eyes.

"Who was the guy on the porch? The guy talking to you when the meeting broke?" I asked.

"Honeybun, I want you to brief me on what you're uncovering about my nasty hog farm enemies," Miss Emmy said, ignoring my question. "We'll have time in the air."

I closed my eyes again and was silent.

"One of those ignoble fuck-ups from the bottom of my barrel," she said. "Is that what you want to hear?"

When I opened my eyes, I saw Miss Emmy yawn. First evidence of frailty I'd seen. Or maybe the second, depending on what happened on that porch. She pulled a Pig Farm beanie over her head and pulled it down to cover her eyes. A sleep mask from Siler.

"Tell you what I'd like to do," I said. "Let's plan on a visit to one of your Barbecue Shacks together. I'd like to try one of your barbecue sandwiches myself and have you show me the operation, back of house."

"A grand idea," Miss Emmy said. She yawned again.

That bought me time. Delay, delay, delay. I scrolled through the contacts in my phone and found a turn-of-the-century number for Delaney-Quinn. I texted the number, identifying myself and asking if this was indeed the correct number for my old friend. I wrote that I had an item of business to discuss.

Iris DeMent's voice came through the airplane's speaker system. She sang about how we'll be all alone when our morning comes around. I fell asleep as she sang about waking up. Wondered if, like she said, I would find all my faults forgiven. I prayed to know that feeling. Prayed for Pearl to find peace, prayed for Pearl to grant me grace, to forgive all my faults.

Chapter Eight

SATURDAY MORNING, OCTOBER 5TH

"I remember I wrote a song about H.F.'s god-awful haircut," Delaney-Quinn said between bites. She'd joined our morning gathering at Pig Farm Tavern.

Ghost had taken the early biscuit duty. Catering for Pearl and Siler and Delaney-Quinn and me.

Pearl had known that by asking for ankle-bracelet range to reach her dad's gravesite, Pig Farm would also be in range. In confinement, her life turned out to be pretty much the same as her unconfined life. Morning walk to the graveyard and back. Afternoon at Pig Farm. Evening at home cooking or writing or listening to music.

Thanks to Ghost, biscuits and cinnamon rolls and wax paper wrappers covered the bar. Siler poured from fresh pots of tea and coffee.

"How did the biscuit song go?" Pearl said.

"I had trouble remembering the lyrics then," Delaney-Quinn said. "I don't have a clue now."

Pearl tore out the center swirl of a cinnamon roll, a promise to herself to eat just one bite – the best bite. Then she glanced at me to let me know she knew I knew that she'd eat the rest in a few minutes.

"The songs were pretty awful, as I recall," Delaney-Quinn said. "I believe H.F. came up with a song about drowning in a bowl of grits. Somebody wrote one about dirty underwear. That had to be Ghost or H.F. Otherwise, I got nothing. No secret files with lyrics."

"Not me," Ghost said. "My briefs sparkle. You could eat off my briefs."

"We're going to need a lot of cider," Siler said.

"I know there was something you were sending out to promote the band," Delaney-Quinn said. "What happened to the demo tape?"

"Yeah, we did," I said. "I'm sure the tape is long gone now. A pile of dust in somebody's attic."

Ghost was writing on a legal pad tucked into his leather folio. Blue ink from the marbled blue Conway Stewart fountain pen.

"Folks, as interesting as the setlist may be to Snow Camp fans everywhere, we need to prep for Tuesday's hearing," Ghost said.

"What's to prep?" Pearl said. "I busted his ribs instead of shooting him full of buckshot. That's my full and complete testimony."

"Don't do the crime if . . ." Siler said.

"Hey, I can do the time," Pearl said, cutting him off. "Dropping that motherfucker to the ground was worth it."

"Well, now I wanna be at this trial," Delaney-Quinn said. "Lassie, this woman is way out of your league."

I nodded. I chewed. Scared for Pearl. Scared of losing her. Too scared to say anything.

"Just like you were out of his league, DQ," Siler said.

"Hey, hey, there are no leagues," I said.

"I like where this is headed," Pearl said.

"If we're going down this road . . ." Ghost said.

"What road?" I said.

"Wait," Pearl said. "I wanna hear about the Lassie James – Delaney-Quinn love affair."

I worked the app on my phone and launched Patsy Cline on the juke. *Crazy* . . . . blasted through the speakers.

"Yeah, crazy as it seems," Delaney-Quinn said, "the Fats story really would make a great movie. I mean I wouldn't want her to profit from it. But I'd go see it."

Delaney-Quinn caught herself. "Pearl, I apologize for bringing up her name. Fats is fucking evil."

It was quiet. We all waited.

"Yeah, well, it never gets any easier," Pearl said. "I like talking with friends about Dad. Talking about him keeps his memory alive. Telling stories. Hearing other people tell me their favorite stories about him."

"What are your favorites," Delaney-Quinn said.

Pearl told about how her father had created an oral history project to find and save stories passed down from families that had lived in Cataloochee, a North Carolina town that's now lost to history, swallowed by the Great Smoky Mountains National Park. Sanders Mallette had interviewed old-timers whose families had worked in logging or moonshine, or both, up until the 1920s. Way back, Cherokee hunted and fished there.

I added that he did something similar to document the community tales and family stories in Seaforth and Pea Ridge when those communities were swept away to make way for Jordan Lake. Sanders Mallette knew everybody would see the pretty lake and never think about the stories of the people and the places underneath their boats and fishing lines. Pearl said he was inspired to do that after reading about Judson, the underwater ghost town lost to progress when TVA engineers dammed the Little Tennessee River to create Fontana Lake. Judson vanished. Pearl's voice broke as she continued.

"I love talking about Dad. And talking about him means talking about Fats. And talking about Lassie. Dad's murder brought Lassie to me. Not saying there is any kind of balancing the scales. It all happened so fast, some days I don't know which parts were real and which parts I dreamed." Her voice trailed off.

Pearl rubbed a tear from her eye. She took a couple of breaths.

"Just look up there," Pearl said.

She pointed to the shelf as she stepped away to the ladies' room.

Siler retrieved a pile of envelopes from the shelf, from beside the shot glasses. All letters Fats had mailed to me in care of Pig Farm since her incarceration for the murder of Pearl's father.

"What on earth could she be writing you about?" Delaney-Quin said.

"Every letter is the same. She's pitching a book and movie deal. Wants me to write it. To make the movie you and everybody want to see," I said. "I've never replied. Letters keep coming."

"Pauley must be losing his mind she's still writing you," Ghost said.

Delaney-Quinn gave us a look.

"Pauley is the FBI guy who put me on the suspect list for Mallette's murder," I said.

"Then Pauley screwed up the investigation by assuming some kind of national security threat," Ghost said. "When Lassie solved the murder and broke the story in *The Post,* Pauley looked bad. Really bad."

Delaney-Quinn started in, "Lassie, I recall reading your account in *The Post.* About Fats coming back to Chapel Hill to donate all this money to the University, right before Malette was murdered on the quad and the other couple was killed on Buttons Road. Then how Fats was sound asleep at the old Franklin hotel, and you pressed her thumb against screen to unlock her phone and used an app to track the history of her electric car to place her at the murder sites . . ."

"Yeah?" I said.

Delaney-Quinn lowered her voice. "I remember wondering whether you two had been screwing right before you decided she was a murderess?"

Siler turned up the volume on the juke.

"A damn good question," Ghost said.

"Careful here, man," Siler said.

"I have no recollection," I said.

I fall to pieces . . . more Patsy from Siler's speakers.

Pearl was back.

"No recollection of what?" she said.

"The Pig Farm body politic is lobbying Lassie for more detail about his dating history than he can reproduce," Ghost said.

"Hey, I can solve that," Pearl said. "I can put him under hypnosis. He'll remember everything."

We licked sugar from our fingers and bathed our hands with wet wipes Siler pulled from behind the bar.

"You can do that?" Ghost said. "Put people under?"

"Sure," Pearl said. She found a chunk of cinnamon roll hidden in the wax paper and ate it. "Studied it years ago. Used it with genealogy projects. Hypnotized people to remember details from childhood experiences with grandparents and great-grandparents."

"So do you think you could put Lassie under and have him remember the Snow Camp tunes?" Ghost said.

"Yeah, yeah, I can do that," Pearl said. "Good thing you guys got me out of jail. You can transcribe the testimony right here."

"Hey," I said.

Before I could object, Siler, Ghost and Delaney-Quinn were telling me why I had to do it. Had to do it for H.F. I had a duty. I had no choice, they all said.

"Besides, what could go wrong?" Siler said.

I shook my head. I pointed to the Bulleit bottle on the shelf.

"Oh, no," Pearl said. "No booze for the subject. Need you clear-headed for this."

"What else do you need?" Ghost said.

Pearl set out her terms. Siler needed to lock up the place, so no customers would walk in and disturb the hypnosis. Needed the jukebox shut down. Lights softened. Needed the others to move away from us, leaving us alone and seated face to face.

"And everybody turn off your fucking phones," Pearl said. "And I mean off, not on mute. One good thing hypnosis has in common with jail. No cell phones allowed."

Ghost found a spot down the bar within earshot. He pulled the cap from his pen. Ready to write.

"Don't you need me to comply, to want to do this?" I said.

I was fearful of losing time. Had long been fearful of anesthesia. Afraid of walking in my sleep. Afraid of what I might say under hypnosis. Afraid of many things, I realized all of a sudden.

Pearl pressed her forehead to mine. She kissed me.

"Do you trust me?" she said in a whisper. "Do you trust me, for better and for worse? Do you trust me with your life?"

"Of course I do," I said.

She was silent. I kissed her cheek.

"Don't ask me anything about Fats," I whispered.

"Shhhh," she said. "Breathe, honeybun. Breathe with me."

Chapter Nine

FEBRUARY 1982

"I've got tickets for the Chromatic Maple show at the Cradle tonight. You wanna go?" I said.

Delaney-Quinn sipped her PBR. She ran her fingers through her red hair to pull it away from her eyes. It fell right back in the same place. Her red hair and hazel eyes were driving me crazy. And her silence! Lord, she just looked right back at me, right through me, when I asked her questions.

"I like it here," she said, finally.

Here with me on a Monday afternoon? Here in Chapel Hill? Here on the wrought-iron porch at The Upper Deck? I had no idea.

"Beef tips on rice and rolls downstairs at The Porthole. Cold beer here on the deck. Unseasonably warm February afternoon," she said. "I like it here."

She took the last puff from a joint. Ran her fingers through her hair again. It fell back in front of her eyes again. Lord, I'd pay a year's tuition to touch her hair.

H.F. emerged from the metal stairs before I worked up the nerve to say anything more about the Cradle show. He'd apparently dodged his shift at the Happy Store, a corner shop with ten newspaper racks out front and cheap beer chilling inside.

"Thought you were working today?" Delaney-Quinn said.

"Switched out. I'll be there overnight," H.F. said. "Gotta enjoy this weather."

"So no band practice?" she said.

Snow Camp, the band our Connor dormmates organized, usually practiced in the hours between midnight and 3 a.m. Siler had somehow acquired a key to the old public television studios in Swain Hall. Snow Camp was working up a set for Springfest, the all-campus party on the lawn fronting Connor, Winston and Alexander dorms. Second Saturday in April. Always the same weekend as the Azalea Festival in Wilmington.

"How about 10 o'clock tonight?" H.F said. "Be nice to rehearse at a decent hour."

Delaney-Quinn confirmed that would work for her. Ghost, Snow Camp's bass player, was inside tending the bar. H.F. went inside to buy another round and tell him about the rehearsal.

"Hey, have fun at the Chromatic show," she said. "Sorry to miss it."

The Snow Camp band rehearsal time had given her an easy out. Easy way to decline the date. I started wondering about the chick in my classical archaeology class, whether she would want to go. Shit. I wished I knew her name. Caroline? I remember her mentioning Spencer Dorm. I remembered her talking about home on Isle La Motte in Vermont. Remembered her Mom was Portuguese. Remembered the electricity in her fingers when she touched my hand and asked me to go with her to see Kurt Vonnegut speak in Memorial Hall. How could I not know her fucking name?

"Meet me at Troll's after rehearsal," Delaney-Quinn said. "I should be there about midnight. First pitcher on me."

Worked for me. I had a friend bartending at Troll's. He let me drink on a tab when the month lasted longer than my money.

Delaney-Quinn's dorm room was upstairs in Connor. The south end of the hall, where the window looked out over the old campground grill sunk into the hard dirt between Connor and Winston dorms. Her corner room had a view out to the back to the old cemetery. Once or twice a month, she'd pull the government-issue desk out of her dorm room and set it up in the hall for a quarters game. Kept the plastic trash pail nearby for the freshmen she knew she'd make throw up.

H.F. approached the table with long-neck PBRs. Ghost had set up a speaker in the window. He viewed his primary job as deejay. Bartending was secondary duty. He worked afternoon shifts. No one trusted him to handle Thursday, Friday or Saturday night crowds.

"Hey, dinner downstairs when I finish up here," Ghost hollered out the window, then: "The Go-Go's!"

Hey, our lips are sealed . . . poured out of the speakers.

H.F. asked about progress on the lyric sheets and charts the band needed for rehearsals. Delaney-Quinn was working on those.

"I've got the charts for the biscuit song and for 'All My Underwear's Dirty.' Should have something later today for 'Old Plank Road,'" she said.

"Sad fucking song, 'Plank Road,'" H.F. said. "Do we really want a death song?"

"Doesn't matter what you want," she said. "Sometimes we pick the songs. Sometimes the songs pick us. This one picked us. And hey, man, you've got that song about dying in your grits. 'Plank Road' is fucking art."

We drank PBR from the longnecks.

"Still working on your song about Maggie," she said. "Oh, should have the chart today for '$2 and a Bad Haircut.'"

Delaney-Quinn laughed at her own song title. She began to sing the lyrics she wrote about H.F. and his mess of a hairdo.

"You forgot the line about how much you like my cherry red lips," H.F. said. The coating of PBR turned his lips to maraschinos.

"Some days I like your lips. Some days I don't," she said.

Ghost swapped out the Go-Go's album for Blondie's *Autoamerican* album. Started on Side 2 with "Do the Dark."

"He's gonna play the whole damn album," I said.

"Yep, straight through. Back to front," Delaney-Quinn said.

"Any luck getting a gig, Lassie? Have you sent out our tape?" H.F. said.

I'd borrowed a Karmann Ghia from a guy in my anthropology class. Regional driving tour to promote the band. I'd pitched Snow Camp and dropped off tapes at 401 Opry House in Fuquay. Halby's and Somethyme in Durham. Purple Horse in Raleigh. No nibbles yet.

"The band needs a better demo tape," I said. "What I'm hearing on the tape doesn't sound like what I'm hearing when I see you guys rehearse."

We drank beer until dark and Ghost finished at the bar. We took the stairs down to The Porthole and ate enough rolls to induce naps. We made it back to Connor to rest up before the night out. Rehearsal session in Swain Hall for them. Cradle show for me.

Later, close to midnight, I left the Cradle with Chromatic Maple's steel drum humming in my ears. The band closed the show with a Santana cover. The Cradle behind me, I couldn't decide whether to call it a night. It would be nice to crash and get some sleep. Or take my chances and head to Troll's.

Life choices.

I chose the longshot over the sure thing. I made the walk to Troll's in search of Delaney-Quinn.

Circled around Jordan's, the fancier bar above the cheap dive where I was headed. Kind of an upstairs-downstairs distinction among Chapel Hill barflies. I could see martini drinkers through the floor-to-ceiling glass. Down the concrete steps to Troll's, steps covered in beer and puke.

Turned left into the bar. First person I saw was Delaney-Quinn. She was alone at a booth, back left corner of the place. Half-empty pitcher on the table. Rosanne Cash on the juke box, a lonesome song in her soul.

I drank the beer she poured into a plastic cup for me. She told me the band had an unusually strong session.

On the juke, a Gram Parsons record followed Cash . . . *ain't no place for a poor boy like me.*

Delaney-Quinn said H.F. had asked a sound engineer friend to hang around. They'd captured the rehearsal on tape. H.F. had the tape. This demo, everyone was sure, would win the band a paying gig.

"For safekeeping, here's a backup," Delaney-Quinn said. She slid a Scotch cassette tape across the table.

I walked the tape over to the bar. Got Country's attention. Put two dollars on the bar. Ordered a fresh pitcher of PBR and asked him to store the cassette in the bar's safe. I watched him turn the dial on the ancient old metal floor safe, the size of a kick drum. He opened the door. Put the cassette in the safe. Closed the door and twisted the dial.

"Can't wait to listen to it," Country said. He picked up my money.

I headed back and set the pitcher on the table. Delaney-Quinn was at the Wurlitzer, studying the choices. Facing away from me. Punching keys to move the motor that flipped 45s onto the turntable so the Sonotone 9T needle would pull music from the grooves. *Memories and drinks . . .*

"Merle," she said. That's all she said.

Delaney-Quinn was wearing Wrangler denim and a Woollen Gym sweatshirt with a tear in the neckline. She turned toward me, looking over her left shoulder. Her long red hair hanging in her eyes. I couldn't see her face. She used the fingers of her left hand to tuck her long hair behind her ear. Hair held its place. She kissed me.

Then 1982 disappeared. I felt Pearl's forehead pressed against mine, and I opened my eyes.

Chapter Ten

SATURDAY MORNING, OCTOBER 5TH

"Pearl is the badass of all badasses," Delaney-Quinn said. "Damn, that was amazing."

"Progress, Lassie, we have progress," Ghost said. He was flipping through notes he'd made on the legal pad.

There at Pig Farm, Pearl had put me under a spell. Ghost reported that I had recalled the song titles from the demo tape. Minutes under hypnosis were lost time for me. I hated losing time. I didn't remember anything.

Ghost read off the particulars. Four of H.F.'s songs, "One Leg Down the Hill," "Maggie Blue," "Don't Let Me Die in My Grits" and "All My Underwear's Dirty."

Four Delaney-Quinn wrote, "Mama Was Right About You," "Old Plank Road," "My Dream House is Not a Mansion Anymore" and "$2 and a Bad Haircut."

And "My Biscuit Baby."

The band was also working on a cover of a Rattlesnake Annie song, "Carolina Blue." I'd remembered Delaney-Quinn's fondness for a line about a woman searching for sunshine.

"And you remembered a few lines from 'Haircut.' You recalled me singing part of the song when we were drinking at The Upper Deck," Delaney-Quinn said.

She took in a breath and sang the lines,

> *Your haircut catastrophe*
> *Makes that face look more pretty*
> *That pretty, pretty face*
> *I want to kiss your face*
> *I want to slap your face*
> *How can the human race*
> *produce that perfect skin*
> *on my idiot boyfriend*

"And you recalled a promising date with Delaney-Quinn. At Troll's," Ghost said.

"Yeah, well," Delaney-Quinn said. "Locating the demo tape is the big news."

"Demo tape? Where is it?" I said.

From his notes, Ghost explained that I stored a backup copy of the demo tape in the safe at Troll's. A bartender there was our contact.

"You called him Country," Pearl said.

"Jay Countryman," Siler said. "Chapel Hill's best bartender."

Before Troll's, Country had booked bands at Town Hall.

"He always had really good weed. Haven't thought of him in years," I said. "Guy had the highest tolerance for chaos I've ever seen. He was close with H.F., as I recall it."

"Always composed," Siler said. "No matter how crazy the bar got, Country didn't blink."

Ghost confirmed H.F.'s connection to Country. He said H.F. left Country $20,000 in his will. So far, Ghost hadn't had any luck finding the guy. After college, Ghost had done legal work for Country. He'd lost touch since then.

"Country was buying the old Turnip Patch Mills," Ghost said. "In Hillsborough. He turned the mill into a live music venue with art studios. I handled the closing for him. He created a fine music hall. Too bad it didn't last."

"That old mill is a battery plant now," Siler said.

"Making batteries for your plug-in car, Lassie," Ghost said.

The battery talk prompted Pearl and Delaney-Quinn to ask Siler for loaner charger cords to refresh their phones.

I was exhausted. Siler re-started the juke. He delivered a glass of rye and a mug of tea. I opted for the genmaicha. The excitement was fading. We were right back where we started. We had nothing that would enable a band to play any of the Snow Camp songs at H.F.'s memorial.

"We're lost here, guys," I said. "We have two or three lines from 'Haircut.' Nothing else. I can talk about the band at the service, share the song titles and talk about the old days. We don't have any lyrics. No charts. Nothing."

"We'll find Country," Siler said.

"Country or no Country," Ghost said, "Tuesday morning is Pearl's probable cause hearing. We need to get to Friendly Lane to prep. Rest of you can ready Pig Farm for a Tuesday night victory party."

Ghost, Pearl and Pearl's ankle bracelet walked out the back door.

"Good vibe here, guys," Delaney-Quinn said. "How long have you had the place?"

"Gift from my great-aunt," Siler said. He tilted his head in my direction. His way of asking me to tell the rest of the legend.

A few years back, a great-aunt died and left Siler 53 acres of useless land. Land was in Randolph County, North Carolina. Clay and rubble. The land failed to perc. No way to install a septic system. No way to develop it. No buyers.

In a conversation one night with a bottle of Gilbey's gin, Siler found a solution.

A pig farm. Or the threat of one. With the waste lagoons, stink and environmental hazards, pig farms were despised. He planned a PR blitz, leading with the announcement of Three Little Pigs Farm.

Siler banked on the idea that news of Three Little Pigs Farm would so outrage the neighbors that they would buy his land. Just to get him out of the county. A variation on the kind of threat Miss Emmy's pig enemies were using. To create heat, Siler brought in marching bands to celebrate swine. He paid for local radio commercials. He spoke before county commission meetings, bragging about the number of hogs he'd raise. Pretty soon, in the middle of the night, lawyers appeared at his door. Delivered a one-time, take-it-or-leave-it offer: End the media circus. Sign on the dotted line or face legal bills that would bankrupt him. Siler signed. The attorney handed him a check for five times what Siler had been hoping to get.

"Forty-eight hours later," Siler said, "I bought this building. The upstairs space here became Pig Farm."

Delaney-Quinn laughed like I remember her laughing when she was stoned in the dorm.

Siler tossed her a Pig Farm beanie.

"It's cold out. I can use this," Delaney-Quinn said. "Thank you for today. It was great to catch up. Let's do it again in 20 years. Or, I guess I'll see you both at H.F.'s service. Shoot me the date when you confirm."

"Can't you stay, doc?" I said.

"Gotta run," she said. "I'm on call tonight. I've got a household to run. Patient notes to write up for next week."

She didn't like the look on my face.

"Lassie, believe it or not, some of us get up in the morning and go to work. Perform professional services. Check in on our children, our neighbors. Clean house and pay bills. Go to sleep. And do it again the next day."

"First I've heard of such a life," I said.

"Ha!" she said.

Delaney-Quinn retrieved her phone from Siler's cord. Picked up her backpack, headed for the door. She stopped. Turned back and walked to my barstool. Her hair fell in front of her face. She tucked the locks behind her left ear. I saw her hazel eyes. She leaned down and kissed my cheek.

"She really is way out of your league. Look after Pearl," she whispered in my ear. "And knock 'em dead on Tuesday."

Katharine Whalen's cover of *Sugar* came on the juke.

Delaney-Quinn put the Pig Farm beanie on her head. Blew Siler a kiss. Walked out of the bar singing along with Katharine. *All that I get from you is honey . . .*

Siler's glance directed my eyes to a spot down the bar. Delaney-Quinn left us a joint.

Chapter Eleven

Sunday morning, October 6th

Leander Harlan was a skinny lawyer who got rich off fat pigs. He lived in 1,100 square feet of ranch house in Dunn, North Carolina, walking distance to the El Diablo diner where he agreed to meet.

"Best country ham in the world is right here in Dunn," he said on the phone when we spoke. "I can smell it from my driveway as I'm talking to you now."

Leander lived in the house where he grew up. His dad had been a cop. His mom a seamstress who took in work at the house. At his public high school, Leander read Fitzgerald's first novel, *This Side of Paradise*, and he set his mind to attend Princeton. His fascination with Princeton led him to discover Hobey Baker. Leander began to imagine himself from the same kind of Main Line family. Imagined himself the same beloved and famous athlete. A tall and gifted kid, Leander excelled at tennis. From Dunn, following his private plan, he won admission to Princeton. There he competed in Ivy League tennis matches and starred in Triangle Club productions. He didn't correct classmates when they wrongly assumed a connection to Justice John Harlan, Princeton Class of 1920, whose portrait hung in Nassau Inn's tap room. After graduating from Columbia Law, Leander made his way to a partnership with Scheurich, Kolb and Ortner, one of the world's largest and priciest law firms.

For 40 years, Leander remained a regular at Dunn Rotary Club meetings. He never mentioned to locals anything about his houses in Gstaad and Topanga Canyon. From his time at Princeton, Leander mastered living a double life. His closets in Dunn were filled with suits from the local Sears. The finest hiking and ski wear filled his other homes.

For years at SKO, Leander led the agribusiness team. Now in retirement, he sold advice to businesses, governments and politicians.

"I listen and observe," he said in our phone call. "I advise. Often my advice to paying clients is to hire a lawyer."

He was in a front booth, visible from the street, when Siler and I approached the entry. He waved through the plate glass.

"Hope it's OK Siler is joining us," I said as we worked through handshakes and took seats. "We're partners on a little bar in Chapel Hill. Siler drove down this morning while I read up on hogs."

From Chapel Hill, the drive had taken about ninety minutes.

"Oh, yes," Leander said. "What's your bar?"

"Pig Farm," Siler said.

"In another era, I'd accuse you of running a *Candid Camera* game with me," he said. "As it is, you've given me a funny story to share with the head of my old firm's Beijing office. He'll want to visit your bar."

"He'd love the place," I said. "Second-story space, long and straight. Sort of a swollen shotgun house. Line of stools running down the patron side of the bar. Easy menu. Seven beers. Seven wines. Seven choices of liquor."

"As if designed by God," Leander said. "Completeness."

We made small talk about Dunn. Heard about Leander's admiration for his father's police work. He talked about his mother teaching him to sew. Siler steered us back to the important stuff.

"China?" Siler said.

"China accounts for, oh, 20 percent of the world's population and consumes 40 percent of the world's pork. China imports millions of tons of American pig. Demand keeps growing," Leander said. "Large farms here in North Carolina might have 15,000 or 25,000 hogs. In the Hubei province, they've got 30-story towers with nearly a million hogs. Still not enough. So, the Chinese buy pig meat from North Carolina and Iowa and places all over the world."

Leander waved the waitress over. Ordered ham biscuits and bowls of grits for the table. She poured coffee for Leander and Siler. I pulled a teabag from my pocket and asked for hot water.

"Mr. Harlan," I said, "I appreciate your openness to a casual conversation on a Sunday morning. Miss Emmy is more a friend than client. She hasn't retained me, and I don't expect her to do so. She's asked me to poke around to see if I might help head off a lawsuit."

"Oh, yes," he said. "As I said on the phone, these days I listen and observe. If that's good enough for my friends, I am happy to share my observations. And Miss Emmy has been a friend for a long time."

I nodded.

"It is my observation," he said, "there are hog farmers, owners of hog processing facilities and pork distributors who are displeased with Miss Emmy's enterprises. What she told you is accurate. I expect some barbecue restauranteurs are displeased as well. This kind of displeasure, in my observation, often leads to a lawsuit."

A plate arrived. It was covered in ham biscuits. Petite things. Each one the size of a ping-pong ball. Siler was first to take a bite. Leander's eyes stretched open. He watched and smiled.

"What do you think? Isn't that the best pig you ever tasted? Nearly 700 million pigs in the world, and the best-tasting pig meat is right here in Dunn," he said.

Siler affirmed the quality. He took another biscuit.

Leander pulled a menu from the metal clip by the window. He pointed to the prices for ham biscuits, barbecue sandwiches and bacon.

"See there. These prices are twice what Miss Emmy charges at her restaurants," he said. "Her restaurant competitors are putting pressure on suppliers to lower prices. This is the only way the restaurants can lower their prices to compete with Miss Emmy's. Put simply, they need to pay less to hog farmers and processors. If the restaurants cannot compete, the door is open for Miss Emmy to swoop in and take those restaurants. Miss Emmy is, you might say, an existential threat to these businesses."

The ham really was terrific. I started on a second biscuit. The hot water turned out to be warm water. The tea wasn't really tea. It was a bag on a string floating in a cup of warm water. The grits were hotter than the water.

"Thank you for the direct explanation," I said. "I didn't expect anything so simple. I guess your explanation makes me wonder about the legal issue in question. What's the cause of action, if that's the right legal term?"

"This is where my advice is for you to hire an attorney," he said. "I no longer hold a license to practice law."

He smiled.

"Fair enough," I said. "For now, I'd love to have your observation."

Leander nodded.

"I don't know that there is anything that a lawyer would describe as a cause of action. There might be. Ask your lawyer. She or he may find one," he said.

A string of Willie Nelson songs played on the El Diablo speakers. Leander had not yet touched the food.

"Well, let me get at this another way. Based on similar situations you've observed in the past, what are the things that cause disagreements to disappear instead of ending up in front of a jury?" I asked.

Leander drank his coffee and made a face that indicated deep thought. A practiced expression.

"Aren't you going to have something?" Siler said.

"Oh, no," Leander said. "I'm a vegetarian. Never touch meat."

Siler took a napkin and wrapped up the rest of the biscuits to go. He set the wrapped treats on the table and proceeded to eat the grits.

"My observation is that litigation is a funny thing, Mr. Battle," Leander said, circling back to my question. "People sue other people when they feel threatened. When they are angry or hurt. When they are scared. Our actions follow our emotions. Or as Willie sings about it, *energy follows thought*. The relevance of any specific law isn't usually the reason for a lawsuit. Feelings give rise to the actions. The people experiencing negative emotions hire people with law licenses to find the cause of action that scratches their itch. Something that reduces the negativity of their emotions. Or, on a good day, helps them experience positive emotions."

"So Miss Emmy is fucked," Siler said.

"You, my friend, speak like a senior partner," Leander said.

"Anything you suggest I convey to Miss Emmy?" I said. "Again, as a friend."

"Encourage her to enjoy life. She'll pay her lawyers. There will be dickering with opposing counsel. Then everyone will find a reasonable resolution. Which may require no change at all in her business. Or it may require some change. The right people eventually get together in the room and work things out. Whatever happens, Miss Emmy has enough money that she will move through her life with minimal disruption," he said.

"I don't believe Miss Emmy shares your equanimity," I said.

"You have answered your own question. The best thing a friend can do for Miss Emmy is to help her find and embrace this equanimity, as you put it," Leander said. "I am happy to share my equanimity with her. There is plenty to go around."

"You're saying there's nothing hinky about her business? Nothing I should dig into?" I said.

Leander smiled. His face changed shape, however slightly. His eyes held secrets. I was certain this was the look he gave his Princeton mates when they teased him about his family connections to the Supreme Court justice. An amount of time passed. It was the customary amount of time a person in conversation pauses before responding to the question. That amount of time passed, and Leander sat without speaking. He drank coffee. He ate a forkful of grits. He smiled. His eyes twinkled like the star in Orion's belt. He could have been a mannequin in the window at Gimbels. Or the hero of a Triangle Club production.

I glanced at Siler. His eyes were closed. He was enjoying the quiet. I joined in. We all sat there. What seemed like hours was minutes. Longer than I've ever sat conversationless in a business meeting.

My buzzing phone broke the trance.

"I'll let you take your call, friend. It was wonderful to meet you," Leander said. He rose from the booth, taking the check with him. He paid at the register. He retrieved his hat from a hook by the door and left the El Diablo—his route on the sidewalk carrying him past our eyeline through the plate glass. No wave this time.

The call was from Pearl. Told her the meeting was not quite what I expected but that it had given me an idea. Explained I would need to be on the road all day and maybe into tomorrow. She requested banana pudding and wished me luck. Siler heard my end of the conversation.

"Tell me what kind of idea came to you from our conversation with that guy," he said.

"He bragged about the quality of the ham. Overdid the sales job, really. He never said anything bad about Miss Emmy's pig. He said this pig is better than her pig—way better. Which is a way of saying Miss Emmy's pig is substandard. Let's get a barbecue sandwich to go. Then hit the road," I said.

Back in the car, we mapped out a route. East to Goldsboro, Ayden and Greenville. Back through the Piedmont with stops in Raleigh and Willow Spring. Onward west to Greensboro, Lexington and Shelby. We'd buy barbecue at the famous restaurants in each town. At a few interstate exits, we'd pick up sandwiches from Miss Emmy's Barbecue Shacks.

"What he told us, without telling us, is that Miss Emmy's barbecue is lousy. Maybe the other joints are selling tenderloin and shoulder cuts. Maybe Miss Emmy is selling ground up snouts and feet," I said.

Siler approved of the approach.

"The emotional hurt he described—that's about Miss Emmy's competitors not getting their due. Like the star player scoring all the points who's pissed off that the rookie on the end of the bench is getting paid more money," Siler said. "Or one restaurant selling Wagyu beef and the other selling Spam and both places calling it steak on the menu."

"Yeah, sorta. We'll label all the samples. Get a cooler to keep it all fresh. Or fresh enough. Find a lab to test the meat. There's gotta be a way to test for what's Grade A pig and what is, well, the ingredients listed on the Potted Meat can in the grocery stores."

Siler called Ghost on his home land line. He received a call back with contacts at a couple of labs experienced with conducting tests in support of litigation. Both were in Raleigh. Calling one place, we hit an impenetrable sclerosis of digital voice prompts. At the other, a human being answered the phone. We explained our interest. Dr. Anthony Biocca called back within the hour and explained an answering service handles his firm's calls twenty-four hours a day, seven days a week.

"We meet the needs of clients," he said.

Dr. Biocca confirmed his lab could do the testing we needed. He said it would take a few weeks for results, maybe longer, given the backlog in his lab. When I sweetened the cash offer, he acknowledged that the process could be accelerated. We promised to drop off samples in a day or two.

"Money for nothing, pigs for free," Siler said, when we clicked off the call with Dr. Biocca.

The cooler filled slowly. A grinding, methodical stop-and-go. We crossed state and county roads and federal highways. At a couple places, we paid the owners hefty premiums to open up after hours. Sunday turned to Monday, and we flirted with sleep at a roadside motel where the carpet in the rooms carried the tint and scent of urine.

Visits to these legendary barbecue joints reminded me how much I love a bouffant. Siler made a study of slaw. On Washington Street in Shelby, we parked across the street from the Don Gibson Theatre and ate hushpup-pies listening to "Oh, Lonesome Me" and "Blue, Blue Day." In a Goldsboro parking lot, a man wrote out on a napkin a Brunswick stew recipe featuring squirrel meat. When we tossed our trash at the Willow Spring 'cue stand, a woman in denim overalls and pink boots retrieved our garbage and sorted out the items that belonged in the recycle bin. Siler swore he heard her singing Tammy Wynette . . . *after all, he's just a man.*

After the last stop in Raleigh on Monday, we dropped the pig at Dr. Bioc-ca's lab and headed back to Chapel Hill with the sweets for Pearl. I dropped Siler off on Gimghoul and texted Miss Emmy when I pulled into Friendly Lane. Shared news of my meeting with Leander. Let her know that this was about highly personal feuds.

"Price of being on top, I guess," she texted back. "Everybody takes their shots. Everybody wants to knock me off the top of pig mountain."

I didn't mention the independent testing I was doing. No mention of test-ing her competition's pig or the testing of Miss Emmy's pig. If I needed the pardon for Pearl, I wanted to have a few cards to play. And I'd grown curious. Like the days on a newspaper desk, I was still chasing a story. This time, a story that might help Pearl.

On my return to Friendly Lane, I set out containers for Pearl. Banana pud-ding incarnations from Ayden, Goldsboro and Raleigh, plus a lemon pie from Lexington. The lemon pie seemed to travel the best.

Pearl left the desserts on the counter. She pulled me into the bedroom. She turned up the volume on a Fiona Apple song, "Slow Like Honey." She undressed me as we danced together. Finished with the last of my clothes, she pulled her dress off over her head. There was no other fabric touching her skin. Pearl leaned her forehead against mine. She brushed the tip of her nose back and forth against mine. She kissed my mouth. Two short kisses. Squeezed my lip between her teeth. She moved my hands to the places on her body she wanted me to touch. The song ended. I heard Pearl's breathing. Her places grew warmer, wetter. From the open window, cool air floated into the room. Pearl fell backward into the bed, pulling me with her. She pressed her cheek against my cheek, her lips touching my ear.

"I love you," she whispered. "You're my biscuit baby."

Chapter Twelve

TUESDAY MORNING, OCTOBER 8TH

"All rise!" the bailiff called out. His baritone silenced the buzzing pews.

In the Chapel Hill courtroom, Tenley stood at the prosecutor's table. She wore a gold knit suit and emerald earrings. Ghost and Pearl stood at the defense table. Pearl wore a sleeveless red dress and a necklace with black Bakelite baubles that we'd bought from an artist on Roanoke Island the day after we got married. Ghost looked less rumpled than usual. Charcoal suit with a two-button jacket, a pressed blue shirt and a necktie garnished with little hot dogs and little hot dog buns.

R&R accepted assistance from the bailiff and climbed the two steps to the bench. Same black robe zipped to the neck. Same Carolina blue bowtie.

"What a joy to have my courtroom filled. So many people with a passion for criminal procedure," R&R said. He exchanged formal greetings with Tenley, Ghost and Pearl. Corn Stalks took their spots in the first pew as before, behind Tenley. Stokes wore a brown suit. Cornelia held steady with a puffy pirate blouse. She wore faded blue jeans tucked into black Lucchese boots stitched with pink and purple swirls.

R&R moved easily through procedural details.

"Miss Tenley, call your first witness," R&R said.

Tenley called University Police Officer Frieda Jenks to the stand. Jenks was the first officer on the scene. Chapel Hill cops who followed made the arrest. Interesting tactical move from Tenley. Holding back her chief witnesses, the arresting officers. Starting with the second-string team.

In her initial questioning, Tenley invited Jenks to describe her credentials, her dozen years on the job, her experience responding to gun incidents, the commendations she'd received.

Then: "Officer Jenks, describe what you observed when you arrived at the scene on Gimghoul Road."

"I observed approximately 250 individuals at the corner of Gimghoul Road and Glandon Drive. Several were agitated. When I saw that Mr. Avery appeared injured, I put in a call for EMT," she said.

"And what information did you gather from witnesses on the scene?" Tenley said.

"Mr. Avery and several other individuals told me that Ms. Pearl Mallette had injured Mr. Avery by striking him with a gun. Mr. Avery and several witnesses described that Ms. Mallette had threatened to shoot Mr. Avery prior to striking him," she said.

"Did Mr. Avery and other witnesses attribute violent behavior to anyone else at the scene?" Tenley said.

"No," Jenks said.

"Did you encounter Ms. Mallette?" Tenley said.

Jenks explained that she walked down Gimghoul Road to Siler's house, where Pearl was seated on a sofa on the porch. The .410 shotgun was broken open. The shotgun was resting on the porch. There were no shells in the gun. There was no ammunition on the porch. Jenks said the Chapel

Hill police arrived approximately 10 minutes later. Two Chapel Hill police officers questioned Pearl, secured the gun, placed Pearl in handcuffs and escorted Pearl to the car. Tenley thanked Jenks and took her seat. Tenley would need to question the Chapel Hill cops about the results of their subsequent searches, which turned up no ammunition in the house.

Ghost passed when R&R offered him a chance to question Jenks.

Tenley then introduced two videos of the events of the morning. The videos were taken with smartphones. Ghost raised no objection. R&R had seen the video already, so it seemed a formality. On the government-issue TV, the grainy smartphone videos were jumpy and contained little to no useful audio. R&R was right. The lousy cinematography did not capture the fear and drama that had been evident in the moment. Besides, by now everyone in the courtroom knew the ending. Stokes was safe and sound and with us in the courtroom. He appeared robust and healthy. The video came off as less dramatic than the standard homemade YouTube videos of people doing stupid things. Maybe Pearl's actions were in the middle of the bell curve of modern stupidity.

"That completes the state's showing," Tenley said. She sat down.

R&R removed his glasses and rubbed his eyes. Tenley's abridged presentation shocked me. I figured a ten percent chance she would call Stokes to testify. I figured a hundred percent chance she'd call the two Chapel Hill Police officers who arrested Pearl. Ghost fiddled with his fountain pen. He leaned in and spoke to Pearl.

Finally, R&R spoke.

"Madame Assistant District Attorney, what additional evidence does the state have to present this morning," R&R said.

He was pretending he didn't hear her correctly, giving her another chance.

Or maybe he didn't.

"None, Your Honor," Tenley said, standing up and sitting down all in one motion.

"Parsimony, Miss Tenley," R&R said. "You have delivered a master class in that virtue. The court is grateful. I see many officers of the court here with us today. It is my wish that more of them might admire and adopt your virtue."

R&R stretched out his arm to hand off his coffee mug to Cyril. The judge shuffled papers and wrote notes with his pen until the coffee cup reappeared, a pillow of steam hovering.

"Mr. Peppers, the court is ready for you. Please call your witness," R&R said.

Ghost moved through the formalities of moving Pearl from defense table to witness stand, the swearing in and articulation of name and address and so on. He had her confirm that the videos presented a generally accurate depiction of the events of October 2nd. Ghost quickly qualified the exchange by noting the video content was accurate only to the extent that it showed events that appeared inside the frame of the cameras and did not show other activities at the scene. R&R nodded to acknowledge the footnote.

Then: "Ms. Mallette, reflecting on the events at Battle Park on October 2nd, why did you take those actions?"

"I acted in self-defense," Pearl said.

"Tell the court more," Ghost said. "In what way did you act in self-defense?"

"The actions you saw on the video. I took those actions to protect life," Pearl said.

Tenley's posture straightened. R&R leaned forward.

"OK. To protect the life of the bitternut hickory tree we saw in the video?" Ghost said.

"Yes," Pearl said.

"OK, OK. Did you also act to protect the many thousands of trees in the 93 acres that make up Battle Park?" Ghost said.

"Yes," Pearl said.

"I want to get this right, Ms. Mallette," Ghost said. "You believe there is a lot of life in that park, in those 93 acres. And that you took action to prevent imminent, even immediate harm that would come to that life. Have I described this accurately?"

"Yes," Pearl said.

"You stood your ground? Would you say that you stood your ground?" Ghost said.

"Yes," Pearl said. "That is accurate."

"Why didn't you retreat, Ms. Mallette?" Ghost said.

"Confronted with aggression, I have no duty to retreat. That's what the law says, I believe. I bear no duty to retreat when aggression is directed at me or when I observe aggression directed to others," Pearl said. "I do not have to run or hide. I may stand and defend myself and others."

Ghost looked in Tenley's direction. She raised no objection. R&R smiled.

"Ms. Mallette, from the many options at hand, why did you respond in the particular way that you did?" Ghost said.

"I chose a response I believed to be reasonable," Pearl said, "a response in my view proportional to the threat."

"On reflection, do you still consider your actions reasonable and proportional to the threat?" Ghost said.

"Yes," Pearl said. Ghost nodded to her to continue. "Both Mr. Avery and the bitternut seem to be doing well."

Laughter from the court watchers.

"Do you believe that you responded with deadly force?" Ghost said.

"No," Pearl said.

"Do you understand why others might perceive your actions as rising to the level of deadly force?" Ghost said.

"Yes," Pearl said.

"If the court were to take that position, that your actions did constitute deadly force, would you still contend that your actions were justified?" Ghost said.

"Yes," Pearl said.

"Ms. Mallette, in self-defense, use of deadly force is reserved for situations where someone is defending one's household. Or when there is a fear of serious bodily harm or loss of life," Ghost said. "The state, quite appropriately in my view, requires a high bar when it comes to using deadly force in acts of self-defense. Now again, the court understands you do not believe you used deadly force. The judge has heard your testimony on that."

Ghost paused and looked toward R&R, who nodded.

Ghost continued: "Remembering now that others may believe your actions on October 2nd did constitute deadly force. How would you explain to them that the deadly force was justified?"

"As I said, I was protecting life, protecting the right to life," Pearl said.

"The lives of the bitternut and the other trees?" Ghost said.

"Yes, but not only," Pearl said.

"Well, what other lives were you protecting?" Ghost said.

"My right to life. Trees produce oxygen that sustains my life. Living proximate to trees is associated with an array of health benefits," Pearl said.

Tenley was on her feet.

"Your Honor," Tenley said. "The state understands the latitude the court offers in a probable cause hearing. Yet I must speak up and object here. Ms. Mallette cannot present herself as The Lorax. She is no expert in plant science."

"The what?" R&R said to Tenley.

R&R looked toward Ghost.

"The state is correct," Ghost said. "Ms. Mallette is an expert on her own life. Regarding plant science, the court should know that my next witness will be Dr. Lelani Jakobsdóttir. Dr. Jakobsdóttir holds a chair in plant biology and climate science, a research post shared jointly by Cornell and Duke. She is prepared to review the science regarding the life-giving and life-sustaining benefits of trees. She will describe the health benefits of living proximate to trees and, in turn, the negative health effects and harms associated with living in areas without trees."

R&R seemed to like that reply.

"The court appreciates Miss Pearl's summary of the science and will hold off on any assessment of the merits until we get to hear from Dr. . . . Dr. J. The good doctor brings with her a surname not found in my Goldsboro phonebook. I trust she will appreciate the abbreviation of her name as preferrable to me mispronouncing said name," R&R said.

"Ms. Mallette, let's wrap up here. You said that you to took action on October 2nd to protect your right to life. Do I have that correct?" Ghost said.

"Yes," Pearl said.

She held up her hand, indicating she had more to add. Pearl reached for the nearby water glass and took a swallow.

"And I took the actions to protect the life of my unborn child. I am pregnant. The loss of 93 acres of trees, the loss of the oxygen they produce and the loss of the associated health benefits the trees provide . . . That represents a threat to my life and a threat to the life of my unborn child," Pearl said. "My child and I, we stood our ground."

Pearl looked my way. Tears ran to the corners of her smile.

Chapter Thirteen

Tenley was on her feet and waving her arms at R&R, objecting and asking for the state to be heard.

Court watchers bunched up into conversations like the pick-a-little ladies in River City.

Ghost remained seated. He put the cap on his Conway Stewart pen. Pearl started to leave the witness stand. When she saw Ghost hold up a hand, she stayed put.

R&R sat still, a stillness he must have mastered watching those all-night fires in the tobacco barns. He was skilled at watching smoke blow by. After a period, energy in the room ebbed. He knew it would. He'd seen it before. He'd seen everything before.

"I have a great-granddaughter who charges me a dollar every time I use my gavel," R&R said. "I appreciate you all working the noises out of your systems and bringing quiet back to my courtroom. The dollar you saved me will end up in the Sutton's till today instead of my great-granddaughter's pocketbook. Which reminds me. Cyril, go ahead and put in my order."

R&R came to Tenley first. "Madame Assistant District Attorney, you have the floor. What do you have for the court?"

She was jabbing the pointer finger of her right hand into the top of her table again and again, up and down, as if she were pulling out a thread.

Twice she started to speak. Syllables fell out of her mouth. No words.

"Nothing, Your Honor," she said, finally. "The state has no objection."

"Anything else with your witness?" R&R said to Ghost.

Ghost affirmed he was out of questions for Pearl. R&R went back to Tenley, inviting her to cross-examine Pearl. Tenley let out a heavy breath and declined to question the witness.

"Mr. Peppers, I believe you have your good doctor ready to call. Let's move that along. See what we can hear from her before my hot dogs arrive," R&R said.

Ghost called Dr. Jakobsdóttir to the stand. Right off, she asked for Ghost to call her Dr. J. It's what her graduate students used, she said. A native of Vik, a tiny town in Iceland, Dr. J held degrees from ETH Zurich and Stanford. She'd been in the double-duty professorship, a chair administered jointly by Duke and Cornell, for eight years. She served as senior advisor to the G8 Climate Change Roundtable and OECD's Inclusive Forum on Carbon Mitigation Approaches.

Ghost paused and asked if Tenley or R&R had any questions for Dr. J before qualifying her as an expert. Tenley passed. R&R asked her if she'd ever had a hot dog from Sutton's and, following her negative reply, R&R directed Cyril to find a remedy.

"Dr. J, what can you tell us about what living near trees does for our health? Or, what living without trees does for your health?" Ghost said.

Dr. J paused.

"The highlights, Doctor. Whatever you want to share," Ghost said.

It was as if Ghost had hit the PLAY button on a science podcast. Dr. J said:

"For some children, living near trees significantly lowers asthma symptoms. The effect holds when we control for moderating factors. *Global Report of Environmental Research & Methods.*"

"Living in neighborhoods with greater tree density reduces rates of heart disease. For every 10 additional trees on a city block, on average, residents experience health improvements that are equivalent to the health improvements associated with an extra $10,000 a year in income. Or to being seven years younger. This one is from *Science and Climate.*"

"From *Australian Annals of Wellbeing & Preventive Medicine:* Loss of trees in residential areas is linked to increased cardiovascular and lower-respiratory illness."

"From the journal *Nandice Population Research:* Presence of more trees is tied to better sleep."

"Dutch researchers report living near trees and green spaces reduces rates of 15 diseases and extends life spans."

Ghost put the cap on his pen and leaned back in his chair.

"Dr. J," R&R said, interrupting. "How many of these . . . these headlines. How many do you have?

"150 or 200," she said. "Give or take."

"Give or take, huh?" R&R said. "I like hearing you talk. I do. I have been aware that some of the sharpest knives in the world are right here in Durham and Chapel Hill. It is a thrill to meet one. A genuine scientist. I am going to give you back some of your time today. There is no need for you to share all 200, give or take, headlines."

Dr. J gave the judge a look, as if asking if she was dismissed.

"I have skipped a step. My apologies. Miss Tenley, do you have any questions for our doctor?" R&R said.

Tenley shook her head. R&R didn't ask for anything more.

"Dr. J, the court thanks you for your contributions today. You are dismissed," R&R said. "And check with Cyril. I believe he has a hot dog for you. Please stand near a tree when you eat it."

R&R nodded to the bailiff. Tenley and Ghost stood. Pearl followed quickly.

"I will see all of you back here at 1:30," R&R said. "After meditating over the Sutton's offerings, I will receive any closing statements from counsel. So long as you all honor the parsimony standard Miss Tenley set this morning. I'll rule on probable cause this afternoon."

Cyril shouted the ceremonial commands associated with the pause in the business of the court.

This time, Pearl didn't run to me. She sat still in her chair. I walked through the swinging gate as the court watchers filed out in the opposite direction. I slid my left hand beneath her long hair and touched the back of her neck. Her skin was wet with sweat. I kissed her on the cheek and whispered in her ear.

"If it's a girl, we're naming her Bougainvillea," I said. "Bougainvillea Battle."

Chapter Fourteen

We spotted Corn Stalks fighting the vending machines in the courthouse basement as we left through a side door. A Zagnut lunch for them.

Ghost, Pearl and I walked across the street to Pig Farm for pimento cheese sandwiches Siler had ordered from the Philpot Lane diner. Siler had been in his usual spot during Pearl's testimony. Standing along the back wall of the courtroom. He was ahead of us and had the sandwiches spread out. I worked the jukebox app while Siler poured genmaicha tea and coffee into mugs pulled from the dishwasher.

The Coasters came up first, singing *Zing! Went the strings of my heart . . .*

Pearl grabbed Ghost's hand. The pair shagged across the tile floor, bumping into the pool table and laughing hard enough Ghost had to catch his breath. The Tams sang through the speakers next . . . *be young, be foolish.*

"How quickly can we get Liquid Pleasure in here for a show?" Ghost said.

"Oh man, did you see Tenley's head spinning?" Ghost said.

"When did you find out?" I said to Pearl. "How long have you known?"

Pearl rolled her eyes.

"Please don't tell me you just perjured yourself to bury Corn Stalks?" I said.

"Don't answer that!" Ghost said to his client.

"No worries, Ghost," Pearl said. "I got the call from my doc Monday morning. I got dressed up and walked over from Friendly Lane to find you, to give you the news. When I saw the bucket truck and the THAI fans, I lost it. Walked over to Siler's house to get his .410. I had helped move Carla and Siler into that house. I knew where I put it. I had stowed it away. I also knew there were no shells in the house. I knew it wasn't loaded."

She ripped off a hunk of sourdough and pimento cheese and inhaled the food.

"I figured I could aim the shotgun up at the bucket, at Doll up in the air, to throw her off script. Didn't think it through, really. Made sense to me at the time. As I was walking toward her bucket truck, I saw Stokes and Cornelia dancing like idiots. By that time, if I'd had the thing loaded, I would have shot him," she said.

"The court will not entertain a hypothetical. Please strike her testimony," Ghost said. He was deep into his sandwich.

"The moment lost, you just never said anything?" Siler said. It was the obvious question. I didn't think I could ask it. For fear of the answer. I was glad Siler put the question to her.

"Well, I didn't want to announce it from the cop car. Or from jail. Once I got out of jail, you guys were on the road with Miss Emmy. Out chasing barbecue sandwiches, fighting pig wars. I figured I would get through today's hearing and tell you then. Hoping we'd be celebrating a win later today," she said.

"You didn't know, either?" I said to Ghost.

"Nope. When we rehearsed the self-defense testimony, Pearl practiced talking about protecting her own life and protecting the lives of the trees," Ghost said.

That made sense. She held the news close. Kept it secured. She and Ghost were not conspiring without me.

Siler switched up the music. Put on the Blues Brothers soundtrack. John Lee Hooker boomed through the speakers.

My phone buzzed. Then Siler's. And Pearl's. Ghost's pockets were still. I gave him a look.

"My phone could be anywhere, man. I have no idea," Ghost said.

Cyril sent the alerts. It was 12:45 p.m. R&R wanted to convene as soon as we could get settled in the courtroom. We left Hooker singing and walked back to the courthouse.

R&R was already on the bench. No "all rise" from Cyril. R&R's strategy was evident. The court watchers heard and would follow his direction to return at 1:30 p.m. R&R was going to wrap up in front of the nearly empty courtroom. Ghost and Pearl at the defense table. Tenley in her spot. Siler on the back wall. I was three pews back of Pearl. Corn Stalks walked in and took their spot just as R&R began to speak.

"I am ready to rule," he said. "Before I do, do either of you have any remarks you'd like to make to the court?"

Clever move from R&R. Made it clear his mind was made up. The two lawyers were smart enough to save their breath.

Cyril motioned for the parties to stand.

"Based on the self-defense claim, I find no probable cause and dismiss the charges. My clerk is writing up the ruling now. I will sign it before I leave today," R&R said.

Pearl leaned her head on Ghost's shoulder.

"Having concluded the formal business here," R&R said, "I'd like to pick up the friendly conversation we started the other day. Miss Pearl, may fortune smile on you and your baby. You used up your nine lives today. If that .410 had had a shell in it, you'd be going away."

Ghost put his hand over Pearl's mouth.

"Listen to your lawyer," R&R said. "When I see you on my porch, we will enjoy the music and will not speak of this. Miss Tenley, you have quite the reputation in this county. The smartest lawyer in a county full of smart lawyers. I have now seen first-hand that you are as smart as they say. Smarter. Thank you, Miss Tenley."

Corn Stalks started to move toward Tenley, eager to debrief. Still wanting justice. I made a move toward the swinging gate.

"Hold tight, everybody," R&R said. "Again, in the spirit of friendly conversation, with no law binding us to anything, I am inviting all of you – Mr. Peppers, Miss Pearl, Mr. Battle, Mr. Avery and Miss Cornelia – to have a cocktail with me at 5:01 p.m. today. It'll be ginger ale for you, Miss Pearl.

"Miss Tenley, I understand you serve at the pleasure of an elected official and you will decide your whereabouts this afternoon based on the best interest of your office. We all understand you hold the option of taking this to the grand jury, which surely would give you an indictment."

Tenley thanked the judge in a tone that made it clear she would be nowhere near this gathering.

"Mr. Siler has kindly offered to host us at his little place on Gimghoul Road," R&R said. Another surprise for me today. "I trust you all know how to find the place."

Chapter Fifteen

S iler sat on his porch and shrugged.

I asked a second time about his apparent back-channel communication to R&R. Nothing. Dumb look on his face.

"Maybe he appreciates my sexy indifference," Siler said.

Pulling supplies and inventory from Pig Farm, plus a few items from his kitchen, Siler had set up a bar on the wraparound porch at his Gimghoul Road house. Too big to call a porch, really. Maybe it's a veranda.

I pointed to the bottle of Bulleit. Siler showed me the home screen of his phone. 4:55 p.m. Nobody drinks before R&R's arrival.

This was the house Fats bought on her return to Chapel Hill. When she was charged with the murder of Pearl's dad and multiple financial crimes, she deeded it to her attorney as payment for services. I bought it from him and gifted it to Siler and Carla. With Carla in Valle Crucis at their mountain house, Siler had the place to himself.

The veranda was plenty big for our group. Ghost and Pearl were in rocking chairs in the bend where the porch curved from front yard to side yard. She'd pulled her foot up to the chair and was rubbing the ankle now freed from the monitor. Ghost and Joansie lived two doors down, between Siler and Battle Park. Pearl's gun-toting walk the other morning took her past their front door. Joansie declined to join R&R's cocktail hour. She'd dropped off homemade snacks as her contribution to the peace process.

Corn Stalks walked up at 4:58 p.m. They were holding hands. They climbed the stairs to the porch. Stopped and looked to the right and saw Siler and me at the bar. Looked left and saw Ghost and Pearl in the bend of the wraparound. Hostiles in both directions. I had a sense of what R&R expected to see when he arrived. I walked over to them and offered my hand. They both shook. Ghost did the same. Pearl waved.

"Baby steps," Ghost said. "Baby steps."

The six of us were standing there when R&R arrived. He walked up the stone path without assistance. He used the handrail to climb to the porch. After checking his watch, he called out to Siler, "Whiskey, young man." He sat in the middle of the sofa that looked out to the garden Siler had cultivated in a quadrant of the front yard. With the house set way back from Gimghoul Road, there was room for stone pathways, ornamental trees and perennials. Lavender cones hung off butterfly bushes. A line of photinia with leaves red as rhubarb stalks. All kinds of herbs.

I fetched R&R's whiskey and took it to him. Ghost and I waved Cornelia and Stokes to the bar. She took coffee and declined Siler's offer to add liquor to the mug. Whiskey sour for Stokes.

Ghost was next. Bulleit Rye, no ice.

I walked over to Pearl. She took my hand, and we walked to the bar. Pellegrino on ice with lime for her. Rye on ice for me. Siler poured himself coffee and added whiskey.

We assembled around R&R at the sofa. Pearl took a seat positioned off one corner of the sofa. Cornelia took the chair at the sofa's opposite end. Conversation was choppy. Weather. Resilience of the exterior paint on Siler's house. Mileage on SUVs. R&R broke through.

"My friends," he said, "how glorious to be on a porch in autumn. With sunset approaching. Meeting all of you good folks has inspired me to reflect on times across my nine decades when I lost or suffered or failed and believed, with all my heart, I would never recover. Believed the world would come to an end. I came to know the only option is onward. Onward. Onward. There is nothing that has occurred between you all that will linger. Just let go. Onward."

"Judge, this isn't fair," Stokes said. "Pearl deserves to be punished. We need justice here."

Pearl sat up straight. Ghost put his hand on her shoulder. R&R drank his glass dry.

"Mr. Avery," R&R said, "I had hoped to avoid delivering a candid assessment. Your comment requires me to share what I had hoped to keep in my heart."

R&R waved his glass. Siler moved to refill it.

"Son," R&R said, waving a hand in Pearl's direction, "this pretty woman whipped your ass. A pretty woman who, we now know, is carrying a child. She reminds me of women I knew in Goldsboro. Hard-boned women. More than one of them whipped my ass. You want to brag about it, son. I held my head high and bragged about the pretty woman that whipped me with a strop when I was twenty years old. Ha! I deserved it. Later, a hard-boned woman whipped me with the long handle of a rake. I showed up on her porch the next day and asked if she'd allow me to clean her gutters."

No one said a word. R&R breathed deep and exhaled.

"Fall air is good medicine," he said.

The judge took a sip from the glass filled again with whiskey.

"Mr. Avery," he said. "Your pursuit of a remedy in court will result in discovery, legal rulings and, if you persist, a formal ruling that she whipped your ass. She will have a pregnant belly out to here when she takes the witness stand. What we have now, right now, is lore, friends. Lore. It can become any story you make it. When Willie Nelson passed out drunk and had a woman sew him up in a bedsheet and beat him with a broomstick, he didn't sue. He told the story. Lore is our friend."

R&R turning Stokes into Willie Nelson. Brilliant.

"On the other hand, if a jury rules and appellate courts print up legal decisions, you will have documented facts in history books. Your legal victory will be your personal loss. Forever more, son, you will be the ass-whipped man they study in law schools. You don't want the court to use all that ink to memorialize on paper that this woman whipped your ass. Keep this your story. Tell it the way you want to tell it. The way you and she tell it together. It's not a story for the court to tell. If it were me, I'd brag on every barstool in the state about how I was the only man who so riled up Miss Pearl that she wrapped a gunstock around my ribs. I'd have Remington pay me to endorse a shotgun. Appear alongside Miss Pearl in glossy magazine advertisements. Make it your story, Mr. Avery."

"Yes, Your Honor," Stokes said.

"Now take everything I've said up to now as you would take advice from your pastor. I also want to offer you an editorial comment, the kind of thing your pastor would not tell you. If Miss Pearl had not whipped your ass last week, ten men were lining up to do so. You don't want to live your life as an ass-whipping magnet, son. You've got a pretty woman who, for now, loves you. If you don't fix yourself, Miss Cornelia will be the one whipping your ass."

R&R finished the second glass of whiskey. He drank the glass dry as he rose from the sofa. He headed down the steps, toward the SUV that would take him to his farm.

From the stone walkway, he turned to speak.

"Miss Pearl, you understand that I cannot speak to a woman in the manner I spoke to Mr. Avery," R&R said. "My great-granddaughters tell me I should address every human being the same. Count my inability to do so among my many failures. Just know that what I said to Mr. Avery does in fact apply to you. Your Battle Park gets mowed down; your life will move on. If Kemp Plummer Battle himself returned to Chapel Hill today, he'd cry tears for all the trees we mowed down since his passing. You would be doing me a personal favor to join Mr. Avery in cleaning up the milk you two spilt."

R&R turned and made his way to the SUV. He used the grab handle to pull himself into the truck and was gone.

For several beats, no one said a word. Siler stepped inside the house and returned with a tray.

"Snacks from Joansie," Siler said. "Her deviled eggs. Celery and radishes with her homemade smashed chickpea dip."

Finally, Cornelia spoke.

"I don't know. It seems like we should ask the DA to do the grand jury thing. Doesn't seem right to let it all go," Cornelia said.

"Understandable," Ghost said. "That would be the customary route from here."

"All we wanted to do was make the park look pretty like Exit 4," Cornelia said. She dipped celery into smashed chickpeas and ate it. Ghost followed her and chomped on vegetables.

Pearl let out a long breath.

"Stokes," she said.

"Yeah?" he said.

"I am sorry I hit you with the .410," Pearl said.

Cornelia's coffee cup was empty. Siler refilled it. This time she added the whiskey. Siler took Stokes's glass and returned with another sour.

Siler brought the bottle around and poured refills for Ghost and for me.

"Thank you, Pearl," Stokes said. "Give me a day or two. I expect I will accept your apology once my ribs stop hurting."

The laughter was forced and unconvincing. Still, it was going better than I expected. Siler punched buttons on his phone and a Lumineers song seeped through the windows to the porch. *It's a long road to wisdom . . .*

Siler nudged the conversation along by inviting Corn Stalks to stop by Pig Farm tomorrow. Ghost jumped in, too.

"Pearl," Ghost said, "you OK with Stokes telling the story his own way? Bragging about being the only man ever set off your temper like that? You all saw there was no court reporter in there. There's no official record of testimony."

Pearl nodded yes. She laughed a little laugh to herself. Her eyes told me she was thinking about a secret she was keeping. Made me wonder about her secret world.

Cornelia softened. Maybe it was the judge. Maybe the fear of having her partner held up to courtroom ridicule. Maybe it was the whiskey.

"I guess the grand jury would mean a bunch more visits to the courthouse.

I'd just as soon be done with that place," she said, chomping a radish disc.

I was scared somebody might mention the Board of Trustees meeting coming up in three days. When Corn Stalks would cast the deciding votes for the University to sell the Kings Mountain land, the Montana land and Battle Park to the benefit of their own development firm. All this the day before University Day, the anniversary of the murder of Pearl's dad.

Cornelia helped keep us away from business.

"Have you got a name in mind for the baby?" Cornelia asked.

"For a girl, Lassie says Bougainvillea," Pearl said. "If it's a boy, I'm thinking it'll be Siler."

Ghost let out a whoop. Not a peep from Siler. No change in expression.

"Why name your little man for Siler?" Ghost asked, before I could utter the question.

"I don't know," Pearl said. She tossed her hair out of her eyes. "He's kind of sexy."

Chapter Sixteen

Pearl found enough goodwill to join the handshakes when Corn Stalks exited.

Siler said Liquid Pleasure was unavailable that evening. Instead, he'd booked Green Gables, a band out of Silk Hope playing covers from Waylon's 1969-1975 albums.

"Beware anyone shouting out a request for a song falling outside those years," Siler said.

The band had an afternoon gig in Pittsboro and would be at Pig Farm for a late show. 11 p.m. start.

Four of us, we moved in four different directions. All prelude to meeting up later at Pig Farm.

Ghost walked to his house.

"Enough with the pimento cheese sandwiches for dinner," Pearl said. She kissed me on the cheek and headed to the car for the drive to Friendly Lane, where she'd create her own menu.

"I'm gonna visit Pearl's tree," I said.

Siler nodded.

"That bitternut is a celebrity," he said. "I'm negotiating to be its agent."

Siler started cocktail-hour cleanup. He packed the items he'd ferry back to Pig Farm.

I wanted time in the park. Its days numbered, I wanted to be in those woods. I entered at Sisters' Corner. Thought about Kemp Plummer Battle walking these trails. On every walk carrying a rock and depositing it at Piney Prospect. From that spot, he had views to the east of Raleigh and Durham.

I thought about all the people walking these woods in the 18th and 19th centuries and the Waldensian stonemasons camping among the trees while they built the nearby castle. Thought about how in my long-ago undergraduate years and again recently I'd walked these Battle Park trails with Fats. Thought about walking Battle Park trails with Siler after Mom and Dad passed.

In the old days, Mom and Dad sometimes joined me for Sunday morning walks here. Poking around in archives, Mom found the first-ever mention of Battle Park in *The Daily Tar Heel*.

"Battle Park is quite a resort these hot afternoons," the student newspaper reported in May 1895.

Dad read up on the legend of Peter Dromgoole and Fanny and the duel for her hand. He knew every detail from Kemp's memoir and made a point on our walks to deliver a rock to the spot where Kemp made his famous pile. Where masons eventually arranged Kemp's stones to form the grand bench.

The whiskey from R&R's cocktail hour was wearing off. I felt the October air on my face. It reminded me of a first date in Battle Park with Hurricane Denise, a left-handed piccolo player in the Tar Heel marching band. She was from Mobile, Alabama. Told me how she fell in love with the wilderness camping on Mudhole Creek on the Tensaw Delta. Homesick for the wilds of Alabama, she'd camp out in Battle Park. She invited me to share her sleeping bag one fall equinox. On the trails, she held my hand and walked us up to trees.

"Shut your eyes," she'd say when we arrived at one of her favorite trees. "Use your other senses to know these trees." She ran fingers down my eyelids to seal them closed.

She taught me to use touch and smell to befriend these trees. To apprehend the hardness and softness of the protective layers, to feel the difference between birch and persimmon.

"Press your cheek against bark," she told me. "Feel the temperature of these living things."

I wanted to hug these trees with Pearl before Corn Stalks built the cabins and lodge and distillery. Before Corn Stalks turned the park into Exit 4. I closed my eyes and rubbed the bark on the bitternut hickory, the site of Pearl's attack on Stokes. I pressed my cheek against it. The bark that fought back, drawing blood from Stokes. I chose a crooked route through the woods. Deer Track Trail to University Trail to Rainy Day Trail. Stopped to visit with a post oak, a swamp chestnut and an ironwood tree. Closed my eyes each time to feel the bark, to touch the leaves. I listened. Held my breath and listened. I wished to hear the trees talk to me, the way they talked to Pearl. The way they talked to Hurricane Denise. I imagined the conversations going on beneath my feet. Tree roots and fungi sharing hydro cocktails.

Reconnected to a segment of Deer Track Trail and took the long way around on Sourwood Loop Trail, walking alongside Battle Branch to reach Forest Theatre. The spot H.F. picked for his memorial service, where Siler would serve his seasonal menu. Reminded me I was failing fast to find the lost Springfest songs. Failing a man's last request. Just as we'd be failing the trees when Corn Stalks showed up with bulldozers.

My phone buzzed with a text from Miss Emmy.

"What secrets have you found about my pig enemies? About my pigne-mies? Ha!"

"Ongoing investigation. More soon," I wrote.

I ignored her series of replies and chose more crooked routes. Park Place to Boundary to Hooper Lane, where the sagging old stone walls joined up to the straight-edged new ones. Then onto a footpath that crossed Battle Lane and carried me behind the University president's residence and to the narrow passage between the arboretum and Chapel of the Cross. A favorite spot. Dessert alley, lined with persimmon, pecan, apricot, pistachio and sugar maple trees. It's where I would find H.F. when he'd disappear from the dorm. He'd tote a blanket to the arboretum and sleep away afternoons. Near his old hideaway, curators had added a piece of public art made from an old whiskey barrel. As good a tombstone for H.F. as any.

Exiting the arboretum, I ran my fingers through the blue-gray needles on weeping cedar limbs. Walked on past the sundial, its inscription reminding me that it's always morning somewhere in the world. I tried to imagine where morning would arrive as the sun set in Chapel Hill. Hanoi? Perth? Walked past the nandina and crossed Franklin Street. Around to Henderson Street and to Pig Farm for the pimento cheese sandwich that I would happily have for dinner the rest of my life.

The juke was running through Siler's selections. Johnny Cash's "Streets of Laredo" was playing on a low volume when I walked in. Placing newly washed glasses on the shelf, Siler was singing the lyrics the two of us had written to the "Streets of Laredo" melody . . . *Last night I dreamed of Rita Moreno.*

The head count at Pig Farm grew slowly. Ghost entered 20 minutes after I took a barstool. Then a foursome for pool. Siler's playlist bounced around.

Kathy Mattea to Joan Baez to Flying Burrito Brothers to Rita Coolidge to Alejandro Escovedo. Siler cranked up the volume . . . *I was summoned by the angels.*

Pearl arrived as Siler was starting the *Red Headed Stranger* album. He lowered the volume. This might be the only album Siler always played straight through. He never cherrypicked one song. Always the entire album or nothing from it at all.

Ghost brought news from a phone conversation with Tenley, who reported that her boss was leaning against going to the grand jury. That was the good news. The not-so-good news: the district attorney wanted to keep the option open. Pearl wasn't in the clear yet.

"So at least you found your phone," I said.

"No, no. No idea where the blasted phone might be right now. Talked on the land line at the house," he said.

Pearl arrived bragging about her dinner of grilled vegetables. Ghost updated her on his conversation with Tenley about the case.

Siler promised to invent a mocktail for her. He called his first attempt a Bougainvillea Fizz.

"Looks like a Carolina Blue Ramos Gin Fizz," Ghost said when Siler delivered the concoction.

"Not quite there," Pearl said after a big sip of blue Curacao syrup, lemon juice, Pellegrino and whipped egg white.

"Nothing but freedom on your horizon," Ghost said.

She did not raise her glass to meet his.

"Yeah, I'm free," she said. "Battle Park is still on death row. The vote is three days away. And the grand jury could still happen."

Pearl traded the blue thing for hot tea. Siler used the search engine app on his phone to look up mocktail recipes.

Ghost recounted his investigator's efforts to find Country. He'd chased leads in Georgia, Montana and, of all places, Warsaw. Best Ghost could tell, Country left town when his Turnip Patch Mills music hall flopped. For a while, Country tended bar and booked bands at the Old Saloon in Emigrant, Montana. He fell hard for a tourist from Poland, a woman visiting the U.S. to see Yellowstone National Park. Country followed her home to the Motherland and got a back-of-house job at the oldest restaurant in the city.

"Place called U Fukiera," Ghost said. "Do not trust my pronunciation."

"A romantic," Pearl said, "following her to Fuck U in Warsaw."

We all nodded. Green Gables was setting up. The sound check served as backing track to Ghost's tale. The good times eventually ended for Country and his Warsaw woman. Two years after his arrival in Poland, he was gone. Ghost tracked Country to no man's land at the shared borders of North Carolina, Georgia and Tennessee. To a rented cabin on Wolf Creek, the Georgia side of the lines.

"If I had to guess, I'd guess he paired up with a landowner to tend a marijuana farm. Either he's dead or he took on another name. The trail for Jay Countryman ends on Wolf Creek. He had easy access to towns and courthouses in three states. He could have been Jay Countryman in one place and anybody else in the other two states.

"Any chance he made it back to Warsaw?" Pearl said.

"Sure, but not under cover of his Jay Countryman passport," Ghost said. "Investigator would find that. And we've contacted the woman in Warsaw. Woman named Victoria Melnyk."

"What did she say?" Pearl said.

"Victoria Melnyk said Country was an above-average kisser with above-average weed," Ghost said, "and if I find him, I should remind the motherfucker he owes her 10,000 zloty. My guy says about $2,200."

Pearl nodded approval to Siler's new mocktail offering, a Mango Mule.

Siler used his wood-handle knife to cut open a new bottle of Bulleit Rye. Poured mine on ice. Poured it neat for Ghost. Poured his into a mug of boiling coffee.

Green Gables opened the show a few minutes ahead of schedule, kicking off with "Yellow Haired Woman" from a 1970 album. Then "Lonely Weekends," a Charlie Rich song Waylon recorded in 1969. Pearl kissed me on the lips. I tasted the cucumber slices from the mocktail garnish. She whispered something in my ear. The music was too loud for me to hear her. I followed her to a spot between the pool table and the band. Pig Farm dance floor. She pulled me close when the band began "Dreaming My Dreams."

Dizzy from the whiskey and the cucumber kiss, I closed my eyes. I saw Pearl in the Maine forest, dancing among the dawn redwoods and white pines. In my mind's dream, the trees danced with Pearl. The tree branches and Pearl kept time with Waylon. Pearl leaned her forehead to mine. She pressed her cheek to mine. I was scared to open my eyes. Afraid to re-enter a world where bad things could happen. Would surely happen. Were about to happen. The last notes of "Frisco Depot" faded. This time I heard Pearl's word in my ears. "Onward," she said. "Onward."

Pearl left for Friendly Lane when the band took a break. Siler, Ghost and I opted for a blurry night with the band. Without anyone saying it, we acknowledged that nights like this had nearly disappeared. Off-the-grid nights between funerals and trials and winter morning walks to visit gravesites. In the blur, I remembered day drinking at The Upper Deck with Ghost and the unexplainable comfort of rolls from The Porthole. Ghost and Siler nodded when I described memories of the old days. Their looks made me realize they had heard me on this already. Had heard me during the minutes Pearl had me hypnotized.

The late hours drew bartenders and wait staff newly clocked out from nearby saloons. Not long after, paper sacks filled with foil-wrapped biscuits arrived. The buttery flour struggled to contain hunks of fried chicken and dripping orange cheese. During the last set break, an argument arose as to whether the shape of the wrapped chicken biscuit creations more closely resembled a mango or a grapefruit. Which led a lanky bartender from the Upsi-Daisy tavern in Carrboro to brag how once he'd thrown a rock to knock a mango off his girlfriend's head. Which provoked a sous-chef from Betty Lou's Tea Room to issue a challenge, to bet the braggart that he could never pull off such a feat. Which led to a quiet-enough-to-hear-a-pin-drop moment where the sous-chef secured a blindfold to cover his eyes and stood down by the far end of the bar, with Siler placing a foil-wrapped chicken biscuit on his head. The Upsi-Daisy bartender selected a four-ball from the pool table, explaining it was ribboned in his favorite color. From 20 feet away, the bartender kissed the ball and then flung the hard resin sphere at the sous-chef's head.

If the four-ball smacking against the biscuit made a sound, no one heard it. As soon as the Upsi-Daisy bartender's aim proved true, at the exact moment when there was certain to be contact with fowl or face, the Green Gables front man was on the mic delivering the opening line of "You Ask Me To." The place erupted in a cheer as loud as anything I've heard since Chris Webber called timeout in New Orleans.

Chapter Seventing

WEDNESDAY, OCTOBER 9TH

I stuck close to the house on Friendly Lane and devoted time to repairing my system's sleep-to-whiskey imbalance. Postponed plans to join the search for Country. Postponed plans to dig for secrets among Miss Emmy's pignemies.

If there had been enough ice in the freezer, I would have dunked my head in a sink of ice water like I'd seen Paul Newman do in the movies. Ended up going the other direction. Scalding shower followed by one, two and three pots of genmaicha tea. By the third pot, my eyes found focus sufficient to check my phone. A text and an email from Dr. Biocca. Paying the bonus had indeed accelerated the research. A report was ready. He explained his lab shared reports only in hard copy form. His lab could not guarantee client-only access once reports were released to the internet's untamable network of servers. The lab's courier service would deliver the report to me at Friendly Lane. Signature required.

I checked in with Ghost. Having slept at Pig Farm, he'd found his way home just after sunup. I was jealous to hear that he'd ordered bags of ice from one of those to-your-door grocery delivery services. The Paul Newman face-first ice bath worked for him. He'd made contact with his pals at the University legal office who confirmed that the Board of Trustees meeting was a go for Friday. Everything moving as planned. Corn Stalks were preparing to file permits that would enable contractors to begin clearing sections of Battle Park. Ghost said he expected the first bulldozers to arrive in the spring.

From last night, I had texts from Miss Emmy asking for "an update on her pigvestigation. Ha!" I sent the same generic reply as before. Investigation ongoing. More soon. At some point, I'd just tell her I struck out. She could deal with her pig foes on her own. Within seconds of sending the text, my phone buzzed with her name on the screen.

"It's time we meet, honeybun," she said, when I clicked on. "I'll text you later with a time and place. Time you share that secret intel you're so good at finding."

She clicked off the call before I could speak.

Pearl found me at the kitchen counter.

She'd been running title searches for the Battle Park land and the Gimghoul Road residential neighborhood.

"Before anyone tears it all down, I'm going to read every line of every text recorded since 1789 to see if there's a covenant, claim or legal angle to stop Corn Stalks," she said. "Either that or show up again with a shotgun when the earthmovers arrive. No waiting period, right."

The first 18 years of my life, most every day my mother reminded me to think before I spoke. This time, finally, I followed her guidance. A knock on the door saved me from commentary.

It was the courier. He waited for me to retrieve my ID and had me sign a document acknowledging my receipt of the sealed envelope containing the report. He used his smartphone to take a photo of me with the sealed envelope.

"Our Dr. Biocca's business must involve more than barbecue sandwiches," Pearl said.

Another knock on the door delayed breaking the seal on the envelope. Siler let himself in before we could answer. Per an alert from Ghost, Siler was delivering three bags of ice. We filled up tanks on both sides of the kitchen sink divider. Ice and tap water to the sink's ledge. We dunked face first at the same time. Stereo Newman. The instant we submerged, we understood that our to-the-brim fill failed to account for physics. Displaced ice and water covered us and the floor. I was out of the dunk first. Siler gave out of breath soon after, coming up for air and sloshing more water and ice onto his front, onto me and onto the floor and the countertop where I'd left Dr. Biocca's envelope.

Pearl grabbed the envelope from the pool. She snapped a photo of the kitchen, now a freezing swampy mess, to memorialize the great ice bath on Friendly Lane. Toweled and dried and drinking from the fourth pot of genmaicha, we opted for a dry table in the den. Dr. Biocca's high-security sealed envelope paid off. Soaked on the outside, the packaging protected the report. I pulled out two pages containing numbered data tables and brief annotations featuring statistical symbols and formulae.

"I was told there would be no chemistry," Siler said.

I looked to Pearl.

"No clue," she said. It's something. It's not English.

Siler took custody of the report and began working a search engine on his phone to decode the Greek. When his battery died, Pearl set him up on her laptop. I called Dr. Biocca. Left a message on voice mail. I pulled together leftovers and served red beans and rice and spanakopita. Pearl started "Froggy Went A-Courtin'" and pulled Siler onto the rug to dance to the Suzy Bogguss song.

Dr. Biocca's name showed on the screen when my phone buzzed. I put him on speaker. Pearl turned down the music. Dr. Biocca called up the report on his computer and walked me through the technical findings. That didn't get help much. He finally realized that he'd inadvertently left off the cover letter, which contained a layman's summary of the findings. He read that to us. Read it twice. No need for him to send a courier with a hard copy.

I pulled clingy plastic wrap off a German chocolate pie a friend had delivered during Pearl's ankle-bracelet days. Between forkfuls of pie, we debriefed on the call with Dr. Biocca. Discussed how to handle the findings with Miss Emmy.

"She's not a paying client. I'm not in her employ," I said. "I paid for the report out of my funds. I can do whatever I want with it."

"Are you going public with it?" Pearl said.

"What is it you want from Miss Emmy? What do you need? Maybe now's the time for horse trading," Siler said.

"Unless one of you needs a pardon I don't know about, there's nothing," I said. "I mean there's stuff I want. Basketball tickets, for sure. Let's make it floor seats in the Smith Center. I'd like to find Country and ask him the whereabouts of that old safe and the demo tape. The things I want are not within Miss Emmy's power to give."

"She might be able to help find Country," Siler said. "I'll ask."

"I have something for her to do," Pearl said.

My phone buzzed with Miss Emmy's name front and center again.

"Good timing. Your ears must be burning, Miss Emmy," I said, phone to my ear. "You are the topic of our table talk."

"Our?" she said.

"Pearl, Siler. Me. At the table eating pie," I said.

"Honeybun, I will set aside the hurt washing over me that you did not invite me to share in your pie."

"You are welcome anytime," I said. "But we have finished the last of today's pie."

"I will hold you to that, honeybun. I called to schedule time with you to talk. 7:30 pm. I will be coming through your town for a private sit-down with a donor. A woman with more money than God herself. Made her first fortune in Arkansas oil and is making her second fortune in green fuel technologies. Got rich burning up the planet and is getting richer cooling it down. Moved to Chapel Hill to be near her grandchild. She's over on Ledge Lane. My car will be at the corner of Henderson and Rosemary at 7:30. My man will open the door for you."

"Miss Emmy, like I said, I don't have a lot to share," I said.

The line was quiet.

"Eugenia, please hang up," she said. She paused again. "Honeybun, our kind district attorney really wants to run unopposed next year. She's asked me for advice. You see, the man who's figuring to run against her owes me a favor or two. Don't fuck with the pink string and sealing wax we used to tidy up this case. The DA could still use a grand jury to stick one or two charges on Pearl."

She clicked off.

At 7:22 p.m., Pearl and I were on the northwest corner of Rosemary and Henderson streets. A campus ministry on the other side of the street. Construction fences and heavy machines on our side. Pearl had scolded me for lying to Miss Emmy about our pie. Pearl would shoot Miss Emmy before she'd lie to her. Pearl wrapped up a hunk of pie and brought it as an offering. We looked up the hill anticipating the governor's car. We could see the entrance to Pig Farm and the edge of campus. Then we saw Corn Stalks. Cornelia and Stokes were leaving Pig Farm. Holding hands, they turned away from us and walked up the street toward campus.

"Oh, fuck," Pearl said, "now they're gonna ruin Pig Farm, too. I really am gonna have to shoot them."

"Not their kind of spot," I said, scrambling to de-escalate this for Pearl. "You heard Siler invite them to stop by. One and done, I'm sure. We won't be running into them there."

As we were looking up the hill, watching Corn Stalks on their romantic walk, Miss Emmy's SUV slowed to a stop behind us. Her driver pulled up on the sidewalk near a sorority parking lot. Miss Emmy stepped out of the back seat to greet us. She wore a black dress and knee-high black boots. A red silk scarf hung off her shoulders. The scarf glowed in the dark.

"Two of you come to see me, it'll be easier to talk here on the sidewalk. I like to see faces when I speak to people," she said. She shivered. "Every time I'm on this street, it reminds me of the '95 shooting."

Pearl thanked Miss Emmy for assisting with the court hearing and offered her the wedge of German chocolate pie. Miss Emmy surprised me by unwrapping it and eating on the spot. No utensils. Her man in the suit came around and handed her a napkin.

"What have you got for me? What about these pig people who are out to get me?" she said between bites.

"Wood chips, Miss Emmy," I said. "The folks running your companies are making your pig go farther by adding filler. Microcrystalline cellulose or cellulose gel or carboxymethyl cellulose or whatever they call it. It's plant fiber. From wood chips."

I paused for a reaction. She ate pie. She nodded for me to continue.

"Nothing harmful, from what I have been reading. Or maybe I should say it's healthier than the fried food and junk food to which it's often added. Again, it's plant fiber. Your people are adding veggie material to pig meat. It's carbon, oxygen, hydrogen. Folks who make and sell processed food love it. It doesn't add any calories. It doesn't change the taste. Doesn't screw up our digestion, at least not any more than the junk food stuff that it's in. Think of it as industrial Hamburger Helper. Stretches the meat. Keeps texture consistent. You make 110 barbecue sandwiches for the cost of 100," I said.

"Keep going, honeybun," she said.

I explained that the same wood pulp filler was probably in the slice of pie Pearl delivered to her. Told her about the wave of media stories a few years back, when the national press reported about the wood-chip filler in burgers, fries, onion rings and tacos sold by the big chains. Made for great headlines. News stories ran about wood pulp in dessert items, cheeses, meats. Everything we buy from fast-food joints.

"I mean you can find articles out there saying the filler is bad for us," I said. "Maybe it is. I can tell you it's used in manufacturing medicines. The tablets and capsules we all take. It's everywhere."

"What's my exposure?" she said.

There should be no risk with the FDA. Miss Emmy's enemies had to know about the filler. They must. It was easy for me to discover, and law firms had access to the world's best researchers. She was facing reputational risk. Embarrassment from a lawsuit and a companion PR effort saying Miss

Emmy's Barbecue was not authentic Carolina 'cue. The negative PR posed a greater threat than the legal action. FTC would be unlikely to call this false advertising.

Miss Emmy opened the door to the truck and spoke to her man briefly.

"So you're saying there is no evidence of Iowa pig meat mingling with my North Carolina pig meat?" she said.

"I don't have any information on that, one way or the other," I said.

"So honeybun, you're saying Leander thinks those bad pig people are going to threaten to run a smear campaign accusing me of breaking a promise. Saying I promised my customers all Carolina pig and then I delivered pig plus filler. That right?" she said. "They're going to say folks can't trust me?"

"That's my read of things," I said.

"What are my options?" Miss Emmy said.

I hadn't given that much thought. On the spot, I imagined three pathways forward. One option would be to do nothing. If and when the smear campaign arrived, she could rest on the Miss Emmy brand. Her track record. Customers had been buying her barbecue for a long time. She could respond to critics by affirming her preparations as industry standard. The proof would be in the customer reviews. Another option would be to adjust her supply chain and processing methods to stop using the filler. This would require price increases, which is what the other pig people wanted. To take away her business advantage on pricing. If the smear campaign arrived, she could present evidence proving the critics wrong. Gotcha, no filler. A third option would be to leave the supply chain and processing as is and go ahead and raise prices. No disruption to her business systems, which would be a big advantage. More than likely, higher revenue. Probably some unhappy customers who'd object to the price changes. She'd lose some brand identity as the place to go for affordable 'cue. And this option would require her legal team to negotiate, to have her pig foes stand down. She would buy peace by raising prices and extracting non-disclosure agreements.

Miss Emmy walked a lap around the SUV. Came back around, stood with us with her hands on her hips. Looked up at the sky.

"That shooting on this quiet street," she said. "All these years later, I still can't believe it."

"What are you thinking, Governor?" I said. "You've been a step ahead of us on this all along. Where are you headed?"

Miss Emmy smiled and reached out and touched my arm.

"What about the other barbecue restaurants in the state. What's in their pig?" she said.

"Comes down to old school versus new," I said. "The places cooking local pigs from local slaughterhouses and cooking the pigs on site over hickory logs, they're serving pig meat and pig meat only. There is no step in the process to introduce filler. For these places, it's kill the pig, cook the pig, eat the pig. No chance for processors to add filler. These are usually small places with one restaurant. One-offs. The larger operations with multiple restaurant locations are navigating the same supply-chain issues as you. Their suppliers are providing processed meat with filler."

Pearl was itching to jump in.

"Pearl, I do hope you do not bet your cash money in poker games," Miss Emmy said. "Unburden yourself, dear. What has your brain bouncing?"

I was hoping she'd ask for help finding Country. Hoping. I was pretty sure Pearl was headed in another direction.

"Miss Emmy, we can help keep all this quiet, keep it out of the press and off social media," Pearl said. "I'm hoping we might help each other. We help you avoid the smear campaign. You help us kill this plan to destroy Battle Park."

Miss Emmy turned back to the SUV and opened the door. This time we heard her. She asked her man to bring her a Lucky Strike. He was quick. She lit up the cigarette and sucked in relief. The lit end glowed like her scarf.

"R&R sends me a carton for Christmas every year. In a good year, I get to December with three or four packs left in the carton. Here we are in October, and I'm on the last pack in my R&R carton. Here I am, shit out of luck," Miss Emmy said.

She smoked. We held steady.

"Pearl, the oldest state university in the country is poised to receive a cash infusion of one billion dollars from the sale of real estate. Millions of families in all 100 counties in this state will benefit for hundreds of years," Miss Emmy said.

Pearl reached out to hold my hand. Miss Emmy's volume increased as she talked.

"I'm sure the folks in Kings Mountain and the folks up in Montana are as wed to their land as you are to the little park over here," Miss Emmy said. "The sympathy I might feel for your impending loss is diminished by the pain I'm feeling as the chambers of my heart swell to pump blood under unreasonable pressure. Pain caused by your threat to run your own smear campaign if I don't protect your dirt. Mind you, what's coming to Battle Park is a deal not of my making. And it bears saying, the big house you bought, the house you gifted to Siler, and Ghost's house, all of you are squatting in the middle of what was virgin forest until not so long ago. Until real estate deals created these Chapel Hill neighborhoods that everybody fusses over today. America is one big real estate deal, honeybun. Jamestown or St. Augustine or the Spanish missions in California or the Disney Fucking World, our foremothers killed trees to make the life you enjoy."

Miss Emmy pinched the Lucky butt with two fingers and sucked in nicotine. Her eyes flickered under the street lamp.

"You know I have to put up with that sociology professor going on TV and talking about how Missy Emmy doesn't cook her pig over hickory anymore. Guess what, honeybun? Now if we went around chain-sawing hickory trees to smoke my pig, you would stick a .410 in my neck," Miss Emmy said. "Now, you two need to know I have enough flint in me that I am not going to have people blackmail me to preserve their neighborhood by demanding I kill exactly the kind of development that created the neighborhood they wish to preserve."

"Miss Emmy, nobody is . . .," I said, not sure where I was headed.

"Shhhh, my honeybun," Miss Emmy said, syrup back in her voice. She stepped toward me and pressed a forefinger on my lips. After a beat, she stepped away and flicked the cigarette butt through the construction site fencing. She put her hands on her hips and arched her back, using the yoga stretch to unleash stress. She took in deep breaths through her nose.

"Hold on, Miss Emmy. Please," I said.

"We're all tired," Miss Emmy said. "A long day in a long year. We all flip a switch and our lightbulbs shine every fucking time. We never bother to ask what fuel is burning on the other end of the wire. What I'm hearing from old friends in Washington has brittled up my nerves. Minds from beyond our shores are increasingly interested in our way of life here. Now you two come at me with a threat."

"Let's talk about this," I said, trying again.

"But I have decided that to wake up tomorrow morning and remember nothing from this encounter except the fine slice of pie you brought to me. That is the memory I choose to take from this," Miss Emmy said.

Pearl reached out to offer a hand.

"You have any more pie with you?" Miss Emmy said to Pearl.

Pearl didn't get a sentence out.

"I didn't think so," Miss Emmy said. She wagged a finger. Her eyes were on me.

"Honeybun, we will talk again. Maybe me, you and Pearl will talk. Maybe us three and the DA."

Chapter Eighteen

FRIDAY, OCTOBER 11TH

"You've told it to me three times," Ghost said, popping his palm three times against the bar. "Every time, it sounds like you attempted to blackmail the governor of North Carolina."

Morning meeting at Pig Farm. We had the place to ourselves. Reached Ghost on his land line last night to schedule the legal consult. Promised breakfast from Sunrise as payment for legal services.

Siler was setting up the bar.

"Any chance Miss Emmy was recording the conversation?" Siler said.

"Oh, fuck," Pearl said.

As usual, Siler's question was on point. Miss Emmy was a step ahead, always. Reasonable chance she now had us on tape. Pearl's intent aside, her remarks sure sounded like blackmail.

"Fucking trustees should be voting about now," Pearl said.

Siler refilled my hot tea. Poured coffee for himself and for Ghost. Pearl stuck with ice water from the tap to wash down a cinnamon roll.

"What was Corn Stalks doing in here the other night?" I said.

Siler cut his eyes in Pearl's direction. Waited to see if she had any slurs to throw before he answered. She focused on her breathing.

"Came in to celebrate," Siler said. "Stokes wanted another whiskey sour. Cornelia has discovered the joy of bourbon in coffee. They had a couple of rounds. Talked about their grand vision for Battle Park."

"What the fuck did you say?" Pearl said. The breathing thing never worked for her.

"I nodded. That's what bartenders do," he said. " We nod. Try me."

"Have you lost your fucking mind?" Pearl said.

Siler leaned on the bar. Dumb look on his face. He nodded.

"A pro's pro," Ghost said.

My phone buzzed. Text from Miss Emmy. "Call me," she wrote.

A phone call came in at the same time. Leander's name showing on the screen. I sent it to voice mail.

"Lassie Fucking James," a loud call arriving from the stairwell. Heard the sound before Gerald Pauley cleared the landing. "Why is it that every time I hear about dead people in North Carolina, I hear your name?"

Same as the first time I met him, FBI Inspector Gerald Pauley showed up wearing an accusatory look and a wilted suit. Our first meeting had been right here at Pig Farm, when he accused me of murdering Sanders Mallette.

"How about some food, Inspector?" I said. "We have plenty."

He made a sound. Harumph. Gray suit, black wingtips, solid Navy tie and white shirt.

"Good morning, Inspector," Ghost said.

"Have you checked your phone?" Pauley said.

"Have no idea where my phone is right now," Ghost said. My phone was buzzing again. Pearl and Siler, same.

Siler offered him a Sunrise sack. Pauley picked through the wrapped items and chose a biscuit with chicken and cheese. Siler poured him coffee. Pauley briefed us as he ate.

Later this morning, at a press conference over at the courthouse, the head of the FBI's counterterrorism unit was going to announce the arrest of Doll and the deaths of Stokes Avery and Cornelia Sloop. The Board of Trustees meeting had been postponed indefinitely. The announcements were part of an ongoing investigation into the China Assets Corporation, or CAC, a sovereign wealth fund managing a portion of the Chinese government's foreign investments. CAC funneled capital to an operating company, China NioMolyTech, a corporation that attracted press over the past year for its role in extracting rare earth minerals from the Congo.

"What the fuck does this have to do with Corn Stalks? With Doll?" Pearl said.

Pauley fished around in the paper sack until he found the last cinnamon roll.

"Hang on," he said, biting into the outer ring of the cinnamon roll and pouring crumbs onto his suit.

CAC ran capital through a series of cutouts, with the cash ultimately landing in the accounts of a Lewes, Delaware, investment fund. It was designed not to be noticed. It operated under the name Swan Valley Fund and was staffed by a single U.S. employee, a woman who had also been arrested this morning. Swan Valley supplied the dark money funding Doll's gubernatorial campaign, which violated laws against foreign meddling in U.S. elections. Swan Valley was also lined up to bankroll the Corn Stalks purchase of the Kings Mountain land and the Montana land and Battle Park.

"But it was never about the cabins and the landscaping," Ghost said.

"Right, counselor," Pauley said.

"It was about mining rare earth minerals, like the Congo?" Pearl said.

"Not exactly. About lithium," Pauley said.

China was securing as many of the world's lithium sources as it could. Eight billion smart phones in the world. Every one of them with a battery that required lithium. That represented just the start. Global production of electric vehicles would reach 400 million in a few years. Battery manufacturing had to catch up. To accelerate production, companies needed reliable sources of materials—including lithium.

For much of the 20th century, a mine in Kings Mountain, North Carolina, produced large supplies of lithium for U.S. manufacturing. New mining companies were now looking to restart the old mine. The land bequest to UNC put lithium-rich land in the hands of the University. The same donor owned Montana land and gifted it to the University upon his death. There's less certainty of finding lithium on the Park County and Sweet Grass County parcels in Montana. CAC and Swan Valley would rather dig more holes and tally misses than dig fewer holes and risk leaving lithium in the ground. The promise of the Thacker Pass mine in Nevada had everybody scrambling to find more lithium stores in the Northern Rockies. Hit or miss, the investment dollars represented rounding errors to a Chinese sovereign wealth fund.

"Then Doll got greedy with Battle Park," Pauley said. "Started bragging to the TV folks about scraping ivory off the University."

CAC and Swan Valley didn't have any understanding of local context. In Kings Mountain, there was already a lithium mine. Montanans had been fighting over mines since before the place became a state. CAC and Swan Valley relied on their local agents, in this case Corn Stalks, to identify promising parcels. CAC was the bank. Swan Valley cut deals on land for mining. Neither had any sense of what 93 acres of beloved forest would mean in a small college town.

"CAC and Swan Valley needed a partner smart enough to pull off transactions and poised enough not to ask questions. They wanted a no-name partner, somebody the press wouldn't notice. Somebody flying below the radar. How else would developers planting trees on interstate exits land a deal like this?"

"And the Battle Park stunt with Doll . . .," I said.

"Yep," Pauley said. "Doll was lined up to give CAC access to the governor's office. Stokes and Cornelia were intended to remain in the shadows. Those two showing up at the Doll rally to boot scoot, to crash a champagne bottle against a tree. Well, that wasn't part of the plan. They drew too much heat for CAC and Swan Valley. They went from stealth to spotlight. "

"Oh, my," Pearl said.

"You're not kidding. Oh, my, indeed," Pauley said. "Pearl, your grandstanding with the shotgun. Every media outlet in the world reported on your stunt with those two developers. From Shanghai to Seoul to Sydney. You and Corn Stalks went viral."

Pauley was nibbling away at the cinnamon roll, swallowing half of the outer rings and transferring the other half to his suit. He waved his mug toward Siler, looking for a refill.

"You mean they killed them? Like the Russians do?" Pearl said.

"The Russians throw people off balconies. Always 20th floor or higher. Precise and standardized training with those guys," Pauley said. "Chinese change it up from murder to murder."

FBI agents had been watching Swan Valley's U.S. accounts and the accounts of Doll and Corn Stalks. With the trustees greenlighting the land deals today, the parties were expected to set a closing date. The FBI had planned to track the funds through the closing transactions and then swoop in to make arrests.

"With CAC taking out Cornelia and Stokes ahead of schedule, we had to move in today," Pauley said. He looked to Ghost. "If we'd stayed on the sidelines, the locals would have been all over your Joansie. She's sent some emails in the last few days that constituted clear and real threats to Stokes and Cornelia."

"You have her emails?" Pearl said.

"Oh, yeah," Pauley said. "We have everybody's emails. We have our own version of Google alerts. When anyone sends an email that includes a word we've flagged, the internet servers send us a copy."

Ghost let out a slow whistle.

"Maybe you can locate Ghost's cell phone," I said.

Siler took another tack. "Can you tell us where Jay Countryman is right now?" he said.

Pauley took out a pen and wrote a note to himself in a U.S. government notepad, adding details Siler supplied.

"Hold on," I said. "Back up. The FBI was always going to kill the transaction. Did I hear you correctly? The University was never going to get the billion dollars."

"Correct," Pauley said.

Covered in crumbs, Pauley returned the last of his cinnamon roll to the wax paper wrapper. A rookie mistake. He'd filled up on the outer rings. Wasted the best part, the sugary center swirl. Wasted the tenderloin of the cinnamon roll.

"So how can we help you, Inspector?" Pearl said.

"Well, I'm headed to the press conference. I wanted to stop by to give you a private briefing. As a courtesy," Pauley said. He dropped his eyes and wiped the back of his hand across his nose as he said it.

We all saw the tell. Siler shifted position and smiled. Ghost saw it and sat up straighter. He let out a laugh.

"As I recall," Ghost said, "the White House has a productive and mutually beneficial relationship with Miss Emmy."

Pauley didn't stop him.

"And Miss Emmy," Ghost continued, "has made it clear that Lassie and Pearl are heroes. She's pulled them onstage to pull in voters."

"I wouldn't go that far. I mean, heroes? Really?" Pauley said.

"Heroes now, for sure. Heroes who helped take down a Chinese-run campaign to elect Doll governor of North Carolina," Ghost said. "That sounds about right? Maybe Pearl's show the other day short-circuited your investigation of CAC's plans to extract minerals from our Tar Heel soil. Maybe. Even so, the FBI wants Miss Emmy and her friends to add juice to the PR wave, now that they've helped save U.S. elections from foreign attacks. Hell, Pearl wrapped a gunstock around Stokes before the Chinese got there to finish him off. Before you could make a move."

"Fuck you, Counselor," Pauley said. He stopped there. Didn't edit or correct Ghost.

"Miss Emmy knows having Lassie onstage helps her approval ratings," Ghost said.

"Approval ratings, yes. Hero, no," Pauley said.

"And you've got orders to show up here to invite Pearl and Lassie to join the FBI brass at the press conference," Ghost said, letting out a whoop. "Tell me I'm wrong."

I checked my phone. Two texts from Miss Emmy asking me to join her at the courthouse for the media thing. Inviting me on behalf of the governor's office and the White House. She said she'd been in talks through the night with the White House and FBI. She had news to share today.

Pauley's face turned white as cinnamon roll icing as I read the text. He had no details about White House interests. He had no information about the White House sending senior staff to Chapel Hill. What a mess Pauley looked, standing there coated in sugar and ignorance.

"You're close, Ghost," I said. "Looks like we get to stand onstage again as props. The White House wants Siler there. I'm guessing the White House will like his sexy indifference."

Siler was leaning on the bar. Dumb look on his face.

"And the White House wants Pearl there, too," I said. "Somebody up there loves the video of her smacking Stokes."

"Hey, text Miss Emmy. Tell her we can help each other here," Pearl said. "I have a new deal to offer."

I worked my phone and relayed the message. Heard back in an instant.

"She says to send your list of demands now. A one-time only deal," I said. "She wants to meet ahead of the press conference to discuss terms."

Pearl talked. I texted her words to Miss Emmy as we all left for the courthouse. We made Ghost our plus-one.

Chapter Nineteen

Inside the largest room in the Chapel Hill courthouse, the town's police chief introduced the head of the State Bureau of Investigation, who introduced a White House official, who sent regards from the President and thanked various people and then introduced a more senior White House official, who introduced somebody important with the FBI, a man in a crumb-free suit, who for twenty-two and a half minutes without blinking and without ever saying *um* or *like* described the arrests and summarized the case and explained how our country was now safe. He stopped talking and didn't introduce anybody. The state attorney general stepped to the mic to start a new thread. She introduced Miss Emmy.

Every turn at the mic was always as good as the first bite of cake for Miss Emmy. She hit all of her applause lines. She introduced Pearl and me, mentioning our role in the events at Battle Park. She called Pearl a hero for standing up to agents of a foreign government. Pearl and I waved. Siler waved when she introduced him. Miss Emmy bragged about all the time she spent in Pig Farm listening to the concerns of working-class voters.

As promised, Miss Emmy satisfied Pearl's demands to protect Battle Park, which included appointing Ghost to a spot on the board of trustees. In one swoop, Miss Emmy took credit for Pearl's idea and wiped Pearl's ultimatum off the board.

Pearl and I had 20 minutes with Miss Emmy before the show started. She said she'd bought peace with her pig enemies. She agreed to quit undercutting her competition on price. Her pig enemies agreed not to sue. Everybody signed papers promising never to speak of wood pulp filler. Pearl gave Miss Emmy her wish list. She was careful to talk about ideas, not demands. Really all she wanted was to fill the board of trustees spots with people who'd protect Battle Park from developers. She outlined several options for Miss Emmy, who nodded the whole time. This told me Miss Emmy had her plan in place already. In the end, Miss Emmy delivered for Pearl and used the press conference to grab more headlines.

"Today reminds us that all of the colors of the rainbow shine at the same time. Today reminds us the lightning that sears us arrives with the rain that nourishes us. Today reminds us that we are capable of feeling pain and joy at the same time," Miss Emmy said, looking toward the ceiling of the courthouse so the TV cameras would capture an image approximating her gazing toward the sky.

"So, on a day of loss and solemn prayer, I am gratified to bring news that represents the best within us, news that demonstrates how we can come together in a united effort on behalf of the people of this state. I am appointing a Chapel Hill attorney, Argus Peppers, and my worthy opponent and noted educator, Dr. Janie Spearman, to fill the two open positions on the UNC Board of Trustees," she said.

Even the VIPs gasped. Miss Emmy used the recess appointments to secure Battle Park's future and to build a bridge to swing voters who might otherwise lean Democrat.

"I have more to share," Miss Emmy continued. "Our good friends at the law firm of Scheurich, Kolb and Ortner have responded with astounding speed to support the great university here in Chapel Hill. As you all have read in the news, a donor's bequest had left the university with substantial land holdings in Kings Mountain and Montana. What you have been reading about in the news was our dream that the sale of this land could generate a billion dollars for the university. Money that would have been used to fund tuition-free education for families in North Carolina through our lifetimes and our children's lifetimes and beyond. The lure of cash was in fact part of a foreign attack on America. Now we are all left to pick up the pieces. The partners of SKO have come through for us. Our SKO friends have confirmed that they are preparing to submit to the university an offer of $430 million for the Kings Mountain and Montana parcels and will donate $20 million to endow a fund for the care and maintenance of Battle Park in perpetuity."

"Only thing left is for her to bring out Jay Countryman," Ghost whispered to me and Pearl.

The Kings Mountain and Montana lithium mines would move ahead, led by SKO clients. Miss Emmy announced that the deal had inspired her to launch a new plan. Starting today, state agencies would begin replacing all gasoline-burning vehicles with electric vehicles. She'd offer grants to local school systems and municipalities that opted to move from gas to electric vehicles.

"North Carolina will free itself from the Saudi oil and gas," she said. "North Carolinians will be driving electric vehicles as we take back our freedom en route to our own green revolution."

I couldn't make out what Pearl whispered to me. From the look in her eyes, I could see what she was thinking.

She got it. She got that we'd decided to destroy Kings Mountain and Montana countryside and all kinds of beautiful spaces. The Congo and other spots around the world. All to extract enough lithium, along with a bunch of other minerals, to make the batteries for our electric cars, the batteries for smart phones and the microchips that made our lives run. The microchips built to serve us. More mines meant fewer trees. All those trees, gone. With some small number of the chopped trees giving our chopped pig that smokey taste. And chopped trees to add wood pulp to the processed meat, to our fried potatoes and frozen milkshakes. Just like when we were thirsty for coal, we took it from West Virginia. Now thirsty for elements from the periodic table, we would take them from whoever had them.

"I know," I said to Pearl. She squeezed my hand.

"Looks like SKO is a front for its China clients, who will extract lithium and then sell it back to us in car batteries," Ghost said. "That is, if the mining pays off."

"And if it doesn't, they'll repurpose the land and build pig farms 30 stories tall," Siler said.

Had no trouble hearing those two. Everybody there with us along the back wall heard Ghost and Siler.

Miss Emmy paused to shuffle her notes. Flipped to a new page of remarks. Before she continued speaking, I swear she looked toward me and winked. Same way that star in Orion's belt winked at me the other night. The kind of wink a friend gives you to say *Hey, watch this* just before a leap from a high dive.

"Finally," Miss Emmy said, the volume of her voice rising, "I am excited to announce that North Carolina, the birthplace of aviation, will be the first state to sign onto the Sustainable Aviation Fuels Global Accords. In partnership with firms in the Research Triangle Park and Bentonville, Arkansas, our state is backing innovation that will capture carbon from industrial plants before the gases are emitted into the atmosphere

—before, mind you, before emissions—and will use a novel type of carbon conversion to turn the potentially harmful pollutants into aviation fuel. We will be using carbon to propel North Carolina into freedom and a green jobs future."

Miss Emmy reached her hands into the air in a victory salute. The post-press-conference schmoozing began. FBI and White House officials left out the back door. State and local officials tried to get reporters to notice them. Others were chirping and chatting and telling one another about what they just saw. Pearl spoke in full voice this time.

"We're going to be driving our electric cars to visit the mountains that are no longer worth visiting because we ruined the mountains by extracting from them the lithium to charge the battery to power the car to transport us to the mountains," Pearl said.

"Maybe there's salvation in that carbon conversion," I said.

I'd never heard of carbon conversion. Didn't know if it was a thing. I had no idea how much of what Miss Emmy announced was real and how much she cooked up last night and this morning after hearing from the FBI about the China threat. My guess is she was channeling Kristofferson's pilgrim, her remarks partly truth and partly fiction. Or maybe we really were Jake and Brett. Maybe her words would lead the people of North Carolina to think it so, to construct truths from a fiction. For anything she announced that failed to materialize, I knew Miss Emmy would explain how one of her opponents killed the deal. Despite Miss Emmy's heroic efforts, the storyline would go, this or that villain would bear the blame.

The prospect of carbon conversion didn't move Pearl.

"We're at the front of the line of offenders. Electric cars. Phones and computers charging at every outlet. Microchips in our appliances.

We've got the treasures of the Congo powering our luxuries. Soon the treasures of Kings Mountain and Montana," she said.

The sea of people in the room mushed and mashed toward the front exit, local officials following reporters. Fans of political theater following the local officials. We moved upstream, toward the back wall. Away from the mosh pit. Found quiet by the back window. We had a clear view of Rosemary and Henderson streets. The spot where we'd met with Miss Emmy and nearly unwound Pearl's legal win. The heavy machines at the construction site were quiet. Somebody waiting on a part or a subcontractor. Somebody waiting on somebody else to finish A before they could do B.

"Hey, that's the site of the old Troll's bar, right?" Pearl said.

Siler, Ghost and I nodded.

"It's like Seaforth," Pearl said. "And Pea Ridge. And Judson. They'll tear down that building and build something new on top. They'll bury all the old stories. Maybe the safe with your Snow Camp demo tape is still down there, ready to be buried under rebar and concrete."

"Not a chance," Ghost said. "Troll's is long gone."

My phone buzzed. Delaney-Quinn had seen the press conference. Her text was filled with emojis representing surprise and curiosity. She wrote out words to say she'd be at Pig Farm after work to get intel from us on the wild events of the day. For now, she'd have to settle for the blue heart emoji I texted back.

"Pearl may be onto something," Siler said. "I mean it's a longshot. Then again, that's all we've got. Longshots."

Whatever came in after Troll's was a series of bars, best we could recall.

Then for a while, the bunker was dead space. Then a head shop for a while. Then one of those coworking spaces.

"Hot desks," Ghost said. "That's what the advertising said."

Then for a time, an idle space inside a fence waiting for construction to commence.

Pearl was out the back door and down the back steps. Ghost, Siler and I followed. When we arrived at the construction site, there was a guy inside the fence wearing a white hard hat marked with scars of debris that hit hat, not head. His protective lid carried the logo of the headache powder Bernard and Council invented in 1906 at a Durham drug store.

"BC," Pearl yelled through the fence. "Hey, BC."

Pearl yelled three or four more times, raising her level with each shout-out. When the guy came over, she explained that we needed his help finding and retrieving an old safe from the basement space in the building.

"This is a demolition job, chief, uh, lady. Not search and recovery," he said. "Whatever's down there is gonna stay there. Once we take down the building, we're filling the hole and grading the site."

"Buried. Just like Pea Ridge," Ghost said. "Damn."

Pearl persisted. Told BC about H.F.'s dying wish. About the search for the safe containing the Snow Camp demo tape. Kept hollering at the back of the man's head. BC didn't acknowledge her.

"How about you help us," Siler said, "for a thousand bucks."

BC turned around. Siler negotiated a half hour inside the job site. Peeled off five or six hundred-dollar bills and some fifties and twenties. BC opened the gate. Found hard hats for Ghost, Siler, Pearl and me. Escorted us around back, to the concrete steps that took us to the building's underneath. To the bunker. Back in time. As we turned into the basement door, a memory flashed into my brain of Delaney-Quinn in a corner booth. I could hear Merle's voice. I could smell piss and PBR. I saw Delaney-Quinn pull her long hair from her face and felt her lips on mine. When she touched my hand, I felt the guitar-string calluses on her fingertips.

"Lassie, you with us?"

Pearl's voice pulled me back into the moment. I saw there were no booths. There was no juke and no Merle. The place had been turned into a warren of cubicles and offices. A poly-office of small and smaller spaces. Some spaces built out with sheet rock, some with plywood, some with particle board. History and shitty carpentry had swallowed whatever had been there in 1982.

BC handed Siler a sledge hammer. We were standing in what would have been the middle of the old bar.

"Do your worst," he said. "Clock is ticking."

Siler's first swing sent up a cloud of sawdust and glue.

"Find another one of those," Pearl said.

Siler and I kicked through the wall he had pierced. That put us into a smaller square space. He smacked the sledge against the wall that we hoped would lead us toward the spot where the bar used to be. Or more precisely, the wall that was behind the old bar. We had always stood on the customer side of the bar. The safe had been behind the bartender, on the floor and up against the cinderblock wall and beneath a shelf that held pitchers.

The next wall put up more resistance. Particle board and plywood with some two-by-fours for support. No pattern to the construction. A few amateurs with a nail gun and boards ginning up tiny workspaces as fast as they could. Pearl, now armed, alternated sledge swings with Siler. Ghost and I tore remnants until there was room enough for us to walk through the wall.

We found a supply closet, an HVAC room and a room that had functioned as the kitchenette for the coworking space. Three cubicles arrayed along the space that once contained the bar. The underground bunker was close to a square shape. These three spaces all shared the north wall, the span of cinderblock that was to Country's back when he was selling us two-dollar pitchers.

Ghost scouted the HVAC room. He had a view of the back wall, floor to ceiling. No safe. Siler took the supply room. He smashed the shelving built along the back wall. Nothing there.

Pearl and I took the kitchenette. Lifeless, windowless space. The co-working, hot-desk revolution snuggled up to claustrophobia. No safe in sight. Deep countertop with cabinets below. Above the countertop space, shelves. I stepped back as Pearl swung the sledge through the shelving for the joy of knocking the upper structure to bits. The plywood splintered and crashed. That left the countertop and cabinets underneath. Clumsy construction. Lots of nails and boards with untrue edges. Pearl was sweating and smiling.

"See you upstairs," Ghost said. "We'll find Country, don't worry. Hate that this was a dead end."

Pearl ignored him and readied the sledge.

"I'm going to talk to BC about a demolition job," Pearl said.

Three blows from Pearl, and half of the countertop and cabinets turned to kindling. Coffee grounds, freed from containers by Pearl's sledge, filled the air. Nothing else under the countertop. Pearl wiped sweat from her forehead and spat out freeze-dried granules. She flung the sledge against the last hunk of intact countertop.

Boom. Steel crashed into steel, leaving Pearl vibrating like a paint shaker. Pearl groaned. The sledge flew out of her hands. We ducked and covered. The calamity drew Siler into the room. He retrieved the eight-pound hammer from the floor.

There it was. Right where Country left it, there was the old safe. Pearl's hunch proved true. The safe and the stories inside it would have been buried and forgotten. We pried away plywood until we could see the front of the metal box in full. The door to the box read "Fischer Steel Safe." Above the script, left of the door's center, was a brass dial and a handle. Gold filigree and a small landscape painting decorated the front of the safe above the dial. Siler pulled out his phone and searched for information that would identify this model. When his phone had no battery life, Pearl handed him her phone and said curse words about lithium. She was opening and closing her hands, trying to find feeling in them after the reverberations from smashing the sledge into the safe.

Ghost returned to check on us. Pearl sent him back upstairs to ask BC to lend us a tape measure. Siler found information online about a safe that looked a lot like the one in front of us.

"Iron and steel," Siler said, reading off the specs.

Single combination. Manufactured 1890. Weight, one thousand pounds. Measurements of our safe matched up with the specs Siler retrieved. Thirty-seven inches tall. Twenty-six inches wide. Thirty-six inches deep. Mounted on wheels. Wheels that hadn't turned a revolution in decades.

The safe sat right there, a petrified tree stump. The definition of an immovable object. Half a ton. Easy to see why people worked around it all these years instead of moving it. Siler's web searching was already turning up horror stories about people who'd tried to move safes. A crane could lift it, but a crane couldn't snake down the steps and through the twisty turns of the basement space. Even if we could wrap a chain around the safe and run the chain up the steps to a suitable lift, there was no clear line of egress for the object. How the hell anyone got the thing down here in the first place, we couldn't figure.

"Gravity," Ghost said.

We all nodded. We were quiet. We were past our allotted time. I was going to have to give BC another grand. Or more. Before anyone could make an official declaration of our defeat, Pearl spoke.

"So which one of you is going to roll it to the door and carry it up the steps?" Pearl said.

Pearl looked at me when she said it.

Chapter Twenty

SATURDAY MORNING, OCTOBER 12TH

At sunup, Pearl and I left Friendly Lane to walk the 4,000 or so feet to her dad's gravesite in the middle of the old cemetery on campus.

"What's a daughter supposed to do on the anniversary of her dad's murder?" Pearl said in a whisper.

We walked. Pearl put her gloved hand in mine. We could see our breath. We walked down Franklin to Raleigh Street, avoiding the McCorkle Place site where her father had been killed. Where today officials would be onstage in regalia for University Day activities. A scaled-down event, muted in the wake of the murder of Corn Stalks. Still, more pageantry than we wanted or needed. Once we were past the tennis courts the cemetery came into view. We held hands walking up the rise to her dad's resting place.

"I believe we are supposed to cry. We are supposed to tell stories about your dad. And cry some more," I said.

That's what we did.

We set candles on Mallette's gravestone and lit the wicks. I ran my hand across the chiseled scroll on the marble. I felt the curves and sharp corners of the letters, *Sanders Arthel Mallette*. Pearl's dad shared a birth date and hometown with Doc Watson. On the chilled stone marker I felt the letters in the epitaph Pearl chose, . . . *times are better there I'm told*. A lyric from Mallette's favorite Doc Watson song, "Deep River Blues."

Pearl told me stories. Told me about her father's failed attempts to learn to sail. How after he ran a sailboat aground at Egg Rock in Maine, he signed a pledge to the family never to captain a sailboat again. The candles burned. We cried and laughed.

I told Pearl about all the times her father somehow knew to call me just when I'd hit a tough spot. In the middle of a bad stretch at work, I would hear from him. His timing was magical. We laughed and cried. Pearl talked about hiking with her dad on the Appalachian Trail, reaching the top of Roan Mountain in early June to experience the awe of rhododendron acres blooming. She talked about the homemade trail mix he created for their hikes. He'd roast peanuts and pecans and sunflower seeds and add chopped, dried apricots. Music Mix, he called it.

From her backpack Pearl pulled her dad's bowed psaltery. He was facile enough with it to join in when the porch pickers got around to folk songs he knew. Pearl remembered him playing "Soldier's Joy," "Shady Grove," "Cedar Mountain Breakdown." Most of all, he loved playing the University's alma mater. Pearl had been practicing. I'd been hearing the choppy notes around the house. She took off her gloves and used her left hand to prop the instrument against her stomach. With her right hand, she ran the bow across the first stringed note. I could see the little round stickers she'd used to mark her route through the strings.

Hark the . . .

She shook out her hands. Took a breath and tried again.

Hark the sound ...

More breaths. A sneeze. Then another try.

Hark the sound of Tar Heel voices . . .

On the seventh or eighth go-round, she matched the bow to the strings and got the sequence correct. Any Tar Heel marching band member would have recognized the melody. Her voice was a whisper.

Hark the sound of Tar Heel voices
Ringing clear and True
Singing Carolina's praises
Shouting N.C.U.

Hail to the brightest Star of all
Clear its radiance shine
Carolina priceless gem,
Receive all praises thine.

When the last string fell still, the cemetery was quiet. The candles and the music and the tears were gone. Pearl's dad was gone. We stood there alone. I felt naked in the cold. I shivered. Pearl zipped up her backpack. She turned north and walked out of the cemetery. I followed. I could hear Pearl's voice. Heard her singing to the ghosts living in her mind. She marched to the words a dying soldier scratched onto the wall of Luther Libby's warehouse in Richmond.

I'm going there to see my father
He said he'd meet me when I come

Pearl reached our front door ahead of me and was in the shower washing off the death by the time I got settled. I wet a dishrag in the kitchen sink with the hottest water I could stand and used both hands to press the hot cotton against my face. I wiped my eyes and blew my nose and tossed the rag in the trash.

I used the alone time to read status reports from BC. Pearl had vetoed leaving the safe behind to be buried forever. When Ghost, Siler and I concluded that H.F would understand if we failed to retrieve the Snow Camp demo tape, she looked at me. Her voice was silent. Her eyes were alive. She talked with her eyes, and I loved that about her. I loved that she could look at me with her eyes to tell me whether she wanted persimmon pudding or chess pie for dessert. She could look at me and use her eyes to tell me to turn the heating blanket up two ticks. When she kissed me, her eyes told me where she wanted me to touch her body.

In that bunker, in the place where I drank two-dollar pitchers of PBR with Siler, Ghost and Delaney-Quinn, Pearl had looked at me. Her eyes told me that we would find a way to defy gravity and good sense and without concern for cost we would get that Fischer safe out of that pit.

My phone was filled with news. Lots of activity. Yet, the safe was still in the bunker.

The owner of the site, duly briefed by BC, reached out to let me know that, upon reflection, he had an interest in collecting antique safes. The one at the bottom of his demolition site would be perfect for his new hobby. I offered a thousand dollars. He asked for ten and took five. Done.

BC let me know that he required compensation for turning a demolition job into a search-and-rescue operation. I offered a thousand dollars. Money on top of the money he'd received yesterday. He texted back a thumbs-up emoji. Done.

Bribery was the easy part. Gravity and physics were less accommodating.

Siler had been down in the bunker all morning. While we were at the gravesite, Siler was formulating a plan. I had emails from him with detailed reports. God love the man. He never asked for a cent.

He had torn away all of the cabinetry and countertops in the room that had served as the kitchen for the coworking space. He'd hauled out the debris and busted out more of the walls, making spaces big enough to walk through. Siler had taken everything but the safe out of the kitchen and demolished enough of the structure to make a sizeable route to the door.

Step 1, Siler explained, was to get the safe from here to there, from its resting spot for the past half-century over to the doorway. He'd figured out this part. He'd rig together two hydraulic dollies. One on each side of the safe. Built-in hydraulic jacks would levitate the safe. It would float in place, Siler said. The rigging could support two tons. Our safe weighed a half-ton. A sixteen-foot ratchet strap would hug the safe and marry one dolly to the other. Siler bragged about something he called phenolic rollers. Wheels hard as bowling balls.

I got to the end of his double-dolly emails and didn't see anything else.

"My phenolic friend, what about Step 2?" I texted him.

I made a pot of tea and started an album, "Jimmie Dale Gilmore with The Wronglers." *Time changes everything* . . . was rolling through the speakers when my phone buzzed with Siler's text reply.

"Good news and bad news on Step 2," he wrote.

When I didn't reply, he proceeded with his explanation.

BC could bring in an excavator outfitted with something called a high-reach demolition boom. A long arm extending from a giant yellow excavator. The arm could bend and reach down into a hole. Sounded like a crane, more or less. Siler's description reminded me of the weeping cedar, its limbs drooping and bending every which way. On the end of the boom, Siler said, we'd attach an orange peel grapple. A claw. The boom would lower the grabber. Its four tines would overtake the safe. Siler said it would work like a giant version of the arcade game where the player tries to lower the claw onto the stuffed toy and lift it to freedom.

Siler sent more detail, winding things back a bit. Before we could lower the boom and grapple to pull out the safe, BC would have to create and then widen a hole that would give the machinery access to the basement. The concrete stairs reaching down to the floor of the bunker offered a small landing. We needed to demolish some of the above-ground structure near the stairwell's edge. That meant paying additional costs for a concrete pulverizer or a hydraulic breaker, or both. We'd start out using one or both of those attachments on the high-reach demolition boom. We'd bust out some of the structure to widen the opening to the bottom of the steps. Clear that debris. Then swap out the attachment on the boom. Use the grapple to lift the safe. All a giant arcade game, Siler said.

"So that's the bad news? The added cost of the excavator, the attachments and the operator's time. That's all on us, right?" I texted to him.

"I can see how you might read it that way," Siler wrote back. "I had filed that under the good news. Hey, BC found us a way. And Ghost is kicking in the $20,000 that H.F. willed to Country. Sorry, I left that out. That will help cover the cost overruns with the delay our little search is costing the contractor. Sorry. I guess that really is part of the bad news. We gotta cover cost overruns for the job."

"You said part of the bad news. Is there more bad news?" I texted back.

The grapple would bring up the safe, Siler said, with the two hydraulic dollies secured to the box by the straps. BC said he could bring up the whole thing, the safe and rigging together. He could set it down right there on Rosemary Street.

"Even with those phenolic rollers, there's no fucking way we're gonna roll that thing up Henderson Street," Siler texted.

Hadn't thought of that. A half-ton safe dangling from a boom. Like the song says, *what goes up must come down.*

"You're gonna have to go buy a truck," Siler texted. "That's the bad news."

Before I could text back that there's gotta be an easier way, I knew he was right. Siler was always right. None of us had access to a vehicle that could accommodate a half-ton safe. If we had the boom set the safe in a rented truck, we'd never get it out. If we set it on the street, it would sit in that spot until the town charged us to remove it. If we set the safe down in a construction vehicle, the contractor would be in possession of it.

"Fuck it," I texted to my buddy. "Tell BC we're a go. Tell BC to keep the meter running. When we're done, put in Country's $20,000 first. Then bill me for the rest. Don't bother with an itemized accounting. Just a waste of time to send me more detail about phenolic oranges. Just send me a bill with one number. One fucking number."

Siler texted back a thumbs-up.

Then another text from Siler with a thumb's down: "Sorry. Forgot to unload all the bad news. Miss Emmy says she can't find a line on Country. She's hit the same dead ends as Ghost."

The pot of genmaicha had grown cold as a gravestone. I poured rye into a glass and added three cubes of ice. I switched up the music and sat in our rocking chair to listen to *The Odessa Tapes*. I thought about Jimmie Dale Gilmore believing for nearly forty years those recordings were lost. Gone. Buried under a lake or buried under rubble or burned up in a fire or ruined by the tears of a woman missing her father. Then one day somebody cleans out a Lubbock closet, and *voila*.

Something I couldn't see when this world was more real to me . . .

My glass was dry.

I walked upstairs. I stopped when I reached the doorway to our room. Pearl was sitting up in bed. Her head tilted back against a stack of pillows piled against the headboard. An ice mask over her eyes. Through her gown, I saw the line of her shoulders, roundness of her hips, softness in her breasts, rebar in her forearms. Her skin unadorned. She'd left her legs unshaven. In those first times we made love, when we got to know each other the way meant-to-be lovers do, she had smiled when I whispered how much I liked running my hands up her legs and feeling days of stubble. She winked and told me if I liked the way her stubble felt on my fingers, I would love how it felt on my lips. She was right. She was always right. Pearl was the most beautiful woman in the world. I watched her. I timed my breathing to hers.

"I miss him," she said.

Chapter Twenty-One

On their third visit to Pig Farm nearing midnight on Saturday, the cops shut down the bar.

Hundreds of drunks crowded the bar and the street hoping to win the thousand-dollar prize Siler promised to pay anyone who could pick the three-number sequence that would open the safe sitting in the bed of the giant black pickup truck parked in the alley.

Siler had monetized our problem. Anyone could pay $5 to buy a chance at the combination. A lottery of sorts. Siler set up a table outside by the truck. Players had to sign in with him, pay the $5 and give Siler the three numbers they believed would open the Fischer safe. Siler registered each combination into a spreadsheet to prevent duplication and to connect each entrant to his or her numbers. Over and over, Siler called out a three-number combination. Pearl turned the dial on the safe to test every entry. The door failed to open every time. The crowd cheered every failure. A locked safe meant the thousand-dollar prize was still out there to be had.

BC showed up and paid $50 to try ten combinations. Ghost tried a few. When Tenley and her wife showed up and put down $100 to buy 20 chances, it was evident the search for Snow Camp's demo tapes had captured the town's interest. A forgotten band. A band meant to be forgotten. A band that was a band for less than 365 days. A band that played a set at Springfest '82, a string of songs no one could remember. Songs no one should remember. Songs that didn't deserve remembering.

Ghost denied calling the local TV folks. Somehow, he knew to show up in his best suit. Turning his weepy eyes to the TV cameras, Ghost delivered enthusiastic interviews on the subject of H.F.'s passing. His eyes puddled as he described how this crowdsourcing effort would help make a dead man's last wish come true: To hold a memorial at Forest Theatre, with the service featuring Snow Camp's original songs. Ghost kept bragging how #LostSpringfestTapes was trending on social media. Ghost had Siler secure a commitment from the boys in Green Gables to perform the Snow Camp songs.

"Except there are no songs. There is no music," I said to Ghost as he chased another TV camera.

The safe gave up no secrets. Siler booked more than $5,000 selling chances. Delaney-Quinn was upstairs picking the music. She had Pig Farm's speakers in the window and was playing a Gin Blossoms album when two cops shut us down. *Empty bottles and regrets always piling up . . .*

The cops demanded we move the truck. Siler and I both speculated that a thousand-pound safe in the back of a truck parked in the alley would be the safest item in town overnight. Unstealable and unbreakable. Cops were as unmoved as the Fischer. They wanted the sideshow gone. For a minute, I thought about asking the cops to impound the safe. Just to see what they'd do. Pearl was a voice of reason. Siler shuttered the bar. Before we pulled the truck away, the two cops each bought numbers and tried to open the safe.

Siler's revenue was a fraction of what I'd spent. I'd written a check to the construction company and checks to BC and the building's owner. In all, an amount of money I immediately erased from my memory.

The tally could have been a down payment on a house. I invited my hippocampus to wash away the memory. Same for the check to the Dodge dealership. Paid for the vehicle and tags and insurance and forgot about the price tag as soon as I drove the truck off the lot. Denial was the only way. Denial and onward, onward. Onward from these transactions. Unless the safe contained gold bars, this would end up a loss. A financial loss, that is. For Pearl's peace of mind, to assure her we'd bury no stories, the money was irrelevant.

Once Pig Farm shut down, I drove the short route to Friendly Lane. Pearl, Siler and Delaney-Quinn followed on foot. Ghost arrived later. He had the good sense to bring a paper sack filled with late-night fare.

Delaney-Quinn took control of the stereo and put on a Molly Tuttle CD. She accepted Pearl's invitation to use our guest bedroom and poured herself another glass of rye.

The white flour and fried chicken and goopy orange cheese grabbed hold of us. Delaney-Quinn started the Damn Tall Buildings *Sleeping Dogs* album and turned the volume low. Pearl and I were on the sofa. She leaned her head on my shoulder. Her eyelids closed and opened and then closed and stayed closed. Siler fell silent in a soft chair as he worked his phone. Ghost had the rocking chair, a *New Yorker* magazine open in his hands. His eyes grew to slits, and he didn't turn a page. Delaney-Quinn found the guest room and closed the door.

I kissed Pearl on her forehead and fell into a twilight. I hung there, between asleep and awake. I dreamed we were in a train's first-class dining car. Walnut chairs tucked under vanilla tablecloths lining both sides of the car. A single red rose in a glass vase on every sill. I could see Cary Grant and Eva Marie Saint at a table, each with a martini glass. Townes Van Zandt and Blaze sat across from each other at another table, glasses of beer in front of both men. I saw Butch and Sundance farther down the line of tables in the dining car, each with a shot glass wet with whiskey. Pearl sat across from me. Bubbles shaped like hearts jittered in champagne coupes set before us. Pearl dipped a diamond necklace in the champagne and put the gems to her lips. In the twilight state, I couldn't tell if we were in a song about a movie or in a movie about a song. At one end of the car, musicians played a tune from Game of Thrones. A Lumineers song, I believe. *thousands of hours just to ride all along . . .*

Pops and snaps brought me back to consciousness.

Ghost was dead asleep in the rocker. Pearl was gone. On the coffee table she'd arranged decorative stones into the shape of a heart. Her goodnight message to me before she climbed into bed. Then I realized the popping and snapping was coming from the kitchen. Siler had filled a griddle with bacon. Half a hog's belly sliced up and in the pan. Woke up to the Pig Farm man cooking pig in my kitchen. Siler looked as banged up as I felt. As banged up as Ghost was going to feel when he rejoined the living. Still wrapped in his best suit, the suit that played a starring role in all the TV interviews, Ghost was covered in crumbs and whiskey stains.

Delaney-Quinn emerged from the guest bedroom having found and used the supplies Pearl stocked for visitors. Delaney-Quinn was showered and scrubbed, her hair dancing as she walked. She smiled as she stretched her arms to the ceiling and yelped approval at Siler's kitchen project.

"If I'd have known you'd be cooking bacon for me like this, I'd have married you back in Connor Dorm," she said.

Pearl appeared at the same time. Glowing and clear-eyed in shorts and a soft gray T-shirt with a UNC Women's Rowing logo. She looked robust enough to power a scull through the Schuylkill.

CHAPTER TWENTY-ONE

Lord help us. The men among us, broken. The women, flourishing.

"How do you like your eggs on Sunday morning?" Pearl asked Delaney-Quinn. "Give Siler your order."

Ghost stirred. Slid out of the rocker and crawled to a spot on the floor that would be his bed for now. I tossed a sofa cushion his way.

"How's our chef?" I said.

Siler smiled. He'd been out early gathering supplies. More than just bacon and eggs. During the night, he said, a vision came to him. He figured out a way to get into the safe. After an early trip to the hardware store and BC's job site, he had the tools needed.

"If Delaney-Quinn will hang around," Siler said, "I'll share the secret to cracking the old Fischer safe."

"Why me?" Delaney-Quinn said. "Why am I suddenly essential personnel to a safecracking job?"

She picked up slices of bacon from the serving tray.

"Because we're going to give that safe a colonoscopy," he said.

Chapter Twenty-Two

SUNDAY, OCTOBER 13TH

Delaney-Quinn was yelling at me in my own house.

"You guys really are idiots. You're lovable. And you're idiots. Somehow, you're both," Delaney-Quinn said. "Every time I start to think you're doing something sweet to honor H.F., you turn into dorm rats again. Why don't you just call a fucking locksmith?"

Siler looked at me. I looked at Ghost, who looked at Siler, who was first to speak.

"Ahh, I think we got this," he said. "Besides, what could go wrong?"

"You know, people leave old safes behind because they are empty. They take the valuable shit with them and leave the thousand-pound safes behind. Have you thought of that? You know the thing is empty," Delaney-Quinn said.

Ghost shrugged. "Let's find out," he said.

We headed out to the driveway. As expected, the Fischer safe and the pick-up truck were unmoved and untampered. Siler had strung extension cords and set up drills. One drill he got from the hardware store. One BC loaned him. Siler described the plan. He'd drill a hole in the safe. Delaney-Quinn would perform the colonoscopy and feed a probe through the hole. The probe had a camera and light. The camera would send images of the locking mechanism to Siler's smartphone. While Delaney-Quinn worked the endoscope, Siler would turn the dial on the front of the safe to line up the gates in the three wheels that would rotate as he spun the dial. When the gates lined up, the bolt would disengage. Just like that, we'd be inside the safe.

"Oh, man," Ghost said, "I gotta get cleaned up and call the TV stations."

Ghost started out on the walk back to his Gimghoul house.

Delaney-Quinn searched for words to describe her assessment of this project. She caught herself when she saw the hope on Pearl's face.

"For you, Pearl, and only for you," Delaney-Quinn said. "As a demonstration of my appreciation for your hospitality here, I will perform a colonoscopy on this safe."

And with that, the safecracking began. Siler tried the BC job site drill for a while. Then traded it out and tried the hardware store drill. Then went back to the job site drill. Finally punctured the lower back corner of the safe. Delaney-Quinn took her turn.

Against all odds, the camera on the tip of the probe produced a reasonable video image. A moving image appeared right there on the screen of Siler's phone. We could see the inside of one of the safe's compartments. Right away, Delaney-Quinn's interest leapt. The safe was not empty. The camera revealed what looked like a folder or envelope. There was writing on the outside.

Reaching through the compartment to the front of the safe, the probe's camera found the back of the safe's door. We saw smooth metal where we had been expecting to see the inner workings of the lock. Siler said we were looking for the locking mechanism, something called a wheel pack. The safe door, it turned out, was like an automobile door. The locking mechanism was in the middle of the door, protected by interior and exterior panels.

Nobody blinked at the failure to find the wheel pack. We were too excited to discover the safe held a treasure.

Siler re-oriented the drill to a spot on the front of the door near the dial. We needed to get the endoscope inside the solid-state unit, a door several inches thick. After a couple of tries, Siler bored out an opening and Delaney-Quinn manipulated the line so that the camera scope found the wheel pack. We could see the three discs rotating this way and that as Siler toggled the dial. It took him a while to get the hang of the safecracking method. Getting gates on three wheels to line up was a tedious puzzle, even with the camera view. The safe required certain numbers of revolutions to the right and to the left before the dial could grab and steer each wheel independently into the correct position.

After several attempts, we took a break. Siler wanted coffee. He debated whether his hand would be steadier with or without whiskey added to the brew. He opted to mainline coffee. Delaney-Quinn departed to the guest room for a yoga break. Pearl searched through the newspaper databases she used for genealogy research to find anything she could on Springfest '82. I didn't have enough ice to do the Paul Newman head dunk in the sink. Instead, I ate more bacon.

When Delaney-Quinn emerged from the yoga break, her hair was brushed and her eyes were clear. She nodded to Siler and headed for the driveway. Fifteen minutes later, as we huddled around the smartphone watching the discs turn, we saw the second gate line up with the first. Running on caffeine and Zen, Siler and Delaney-Quinn found magic. With his hand on the dial and hers on the probe, they lured the third gate into alignment with the first and second. For the first time in decades, the gates on the old Fischer agreed. The bolt slid into the opening as reliably as the serpent's shadow finds the Castillo pyramid every equinox. With the tiniest polite click, the safe dropped its defenses. Siler removed the scope and stepped back. Delaney-Quinn turned the handle and pulled open the door.

There was a brown envelope in the larger of the two lower compartments. A sealed envelope large enough to secure standard 8.5-by-11-inch papers without folding them. Delaney-Quinn retrieved the envelope. She led us back inside the house. We gathered around the breakfast bar in the kitchen.

Delaney-Quinn placed the envelope beside the tray of bacon. Written in blue ink on one side was Jay Countryman's name.

"Is it OK to open it?" Pearl said. "It's got his name on it."

"It's like the Klipsch speakers," Siler said. "I put in a blind bid on an abandoned storage unit. Sight unseen. Everything in the unit is now mine. Same here. Lassie bought the Fischer safe. It's his. Its contents are his. And yours."

Pearl looked at me. I picked up the envelope and used a steak knife from butcher block to create an incision. The papers I pulled from the envelope were covered in orange swirls and black ink. No demo tape. No lyrics. Nothing on Snow Camp or Springfest '82.

"Fuck," Delaney-Quinn said. "What are those? Legal documents?"

I tossed the papers on the countertop and grabbed another slice of bacon. A morning of bacon and blues. I found my phone and started a string of Little Walter tunes. I turned up the Bluetooth speakers when I heard Little Walter's harmonica. *I'm just your fool . . .*

Siler lit up high heat under a kettle. Delaney-Quinn headed to the guest bedroom to organize herself for the drive back to Raleigh.

Pearl opened her laptop and searched for a local facility that recycles electronics.

"You guys, dig out any old phones you've got lying around and send them my way" Pearl said. "We've got a bunch of them in a junk drawer. I'm going to recycle them and repurpose a little lithium. And whatever rare earth minerals are in the circuits and chips."

Ghost was back. Walking by the bed of the Dodge truck, he'd spotted the door swung open on the safe. He entered the house without knocking.

"Where's the goods?" Ghost said. "My TV friend said to text her when we struck gold. Somebody lend me a phone."

"Nothing but some of Country's old legal papers," Delaney-Quinn said, returning to the kitchen with her pocketbook hanging from her shoulder. She handed Ghost the papers. "Snow Camp mysteries survived our procedure."

Little Walter kept singing. ... *something I don't understand.*

Ghost let out a whoop.

"God bless Jay Countryman," Ghost said. He grabbed Delaney-Quinn's hand and danced.

God bless Ghost. He identified the documents. Those inky orange swirls decorated certificates of common stock from The Home Depot. There were three pages. Each dated 10 December 1982. Each showing one thousand shares. Each one showing the purchase price at seventeen cents per share.

"Five hundred and ten dollars," Delaney-Quinn said. "If my math is right."

"Think time capsule," Ghost said. "That's five hundred and ten dollars as of December 1982. With today's stock price, it comes to . . . ." Ghost borrowed Pearl's phone and clicked on the browser. He searched for a current quote for The Home Depot stock.

"But this is worthless, right? Aren't old stock certificates worthless? Everything is held in computer accounts now," Pearl said.

Ghost found the stock price and used the calculator app to figure current value of three thousand shares.

". . . it comes to $1.3 million," Ghost said. "As of Friday's market close."

"How much did you spend to salvage this safe?" Delaney-Quin said.

Siler laughed.

"I have no idea," I said.

Ghost borrowed a phone to text his TV friend that the search was a bust. Stand down, he said, no headlines here. We all agreed this was not a matter for the local news.

Siler texted Miss Emmy. Given her fondness for the man, I knew he'd break through the clutter in her phone. She responded right away. She'd had her folks running U.S. and global checks. Still no sign of Jay Countryman. No living relatives. As with our own search, her people tracked Country's trail to Wolf Creek, on the Georgia side of the border, close by the North Carolina and Tennessee lines. No man's land. Siler read off the news from Miss Emmy. I noticed Siler went back to his text editor. I wondered about his additional line of inquiry. Before I could ask, Pearl was sending a request to Pauley. We all knew Pearl would be the only one from our group he'd acknowledge. A half-hour later, Pauley replied. He'd found the same dead end. Jay Countryman's trail died at Wolf Creek. FBI found no relatives.

Ghost used Pearl's phone to videotape depositions, committing to video the accounts from Siler, Pearl, Delaney-Quinn and me. He took possession of the stock certificates. He'd dig into the legal issues associated with possession and chain of custody of such an asset. He'd figure out whether the shares had been sold through a digital transaction, leaving behind paper certificates as showpieces. Ghost would talk with a tax attorney to figure out my options for holding or liquidating the asset. That is, if the certificates still functioned as bearer shares. Federal and state tax offices would take a keen interest. I was happy for the paperwork to be in his hands.

Not long after, a big SUV with military-grade window tinting stopped at the edge of our driveway. Driver blew the horn. Siler went out to handle business and returned with boxes of takeout pig plates from Miss Emmy's Barbecue Shack. The man knew how to work.

"What a dumb-luck windfall with the stock," Delaney-Quinn said. "If it pans out, I'd say that makes up for missing out on Snow Camp songs."

"What about the locked compartment?" Ghost said. "I fiddled with the little door when I came up the driveway. It's shut tight."

Pearl was out the door first, back to the safe. Ghost was correct. So excited to retrieve the sealed envelope, we'd cut short our inspection of the safe. Above the two large open-faced compartments, there was a horizontal shelf partitioned into thirds. The upper right and middle compartments were also open-faced. We could see those were empty. A locked door protected access to the upper left cubbyhole. Siler used one of his big drills to destroy the keylock.

Pearl's hand was first into the space. When she pulled her hand back, she held a guitar pick, a collection of papers folded into thirds, as if prepared for a #10 envelope, and a cassette tape.

Chapter Twenty-Three

"Look at these lyrics. I can't believe we got up on stage and performed these songs at Springfest," Delaney-Quinn said.

We had spread out the twelve loose-leaf pages on the kitchen counter. The Snow Camp catalogue was scattered among clamshell containers of Miss Emmy's banana pudding.

"I find charm in these," Ghost said. "You and I and H.F. had the makings of a real band. Just never found the right drummer."

Nine of the pages contained the lyrics to the Snow Camp songs. All in Delaney-Quinn's handwriting.

Pearl confirmed the titles I recounted under hypnosis matched the titles on the pages.

"I guess 'Plank Road' is okay," Delaney-Quinn said. "I have no idea why as a college sophomore I was writing a dirge."

The tenth page in the stack contained Delaney-Quinn's handwritten draft of the liner notes for the imagined Snow Camp album. We all believed the studio recording session was certain to materialize, with the album falling out of the sky soon after. The notes credited me as van driver for Snow Camp. Credited my mom for supplying cheese straws.

The liner notes reminded us we'd been ready to promote The Porthole as the official restaurant of the Snow Camp band.

Delaney-Quinn's scribbles included three alternative names the band considered. Cane Creek. Silk Hope. Plainfield Friends. She'd marked through each of these choices.

The eleventh and twelfth pages contained two mock-ups for the cover art of the imagined Snow Camp album. Delaney-Quinn had added a note to credit an art major named Teri for the creative work. Delaney-Quinn remembered Teri as her third-floor roommate for one year.

"What the fuck?" Delaney-Quinn said. She held up the drawings for us to see.

"I believe that one is a sunrise. Or a sunset. Hard to tell with black marker drawings," Pearl said.

"I believe the other one is a stylized depiction of the old cemetery," Ghost said.

"Yeah," Delaney-Quinn said, "that would have been the view from our dorm room. Maybe 'Plank Road' inspired this cover design."

Ghost, Pearl and I were nudging Delaney-Quinn to sing one for us. She said she'd rather perform a colonoscopy right there in my kitchen. Ghost and I leapt at her offer. Siler showed up at the house with a cassette player before anyone's pants fell. He'd dug out the boom box from storage in his basement.

"Wait, wait," Ghost said. Still with Pearl's phone, he was reading from a web page devoted to restoration of music recordings. "Says we have to bake them first. Or else old tapes will disintegrate when we try to play them. Tape will turn to dust."

He read to us about sticky shed syndrome. Like how our bones get brittle when we get old. He said old music recordings from the 1970s and 1980s deteriorate. Over time, the tapes would hold moisture, screwing up the magnetic coating. Especially a problem with Ampex and Scotch brand tapes.

"What's our tape?" Ghost said.

"Scotch brand is on the label," Siler said. "There is a 3M logo, and the word 'dynarange.' Also says C-120."

Ghost instructed Siler to set the oven to 130 degrees. He said we'd bake the tape for eight hours. Once it was baked, he said, we'd need to find a machine or a studio to duplicate the tape for us.

"We may only get a single play from this," Ghost said. "It really is a treasure."

We all stared at the oven. Watched it preheat. Siler placed the cassette tape on a cookie sheet. We waited.

The Little Walter music was gone. House was silent except for the tick, tick, tick of the oven's heating element rising to 130 degrees.

"Stop," Delaney-Quinn yelled out. She was running her own web searches and looking at her phone.

"You guys are about to be less lovable and more idiot," Delaney-Quinn said. "Lovable enough to crack the safe and find the lost demo tape. And stupid enough to put a plastic cassette in an oven."

She overruled Ghost. She explained that the baking process was required for high-end reel-to-reel tapes that studios used to record and store music. Over-the-counter commercial cassettes would be fine.

"All that'll happen with baking the thing is you'll melt the fucking cassette and ruin the Snow Camp demo tape," Delaney-Quinn said. "Then again, given our musical talent, maybe that would be best."

Pearl snatched the demo tape from the cookie sheet. Siler replaced it with a bunch of Miss Emmy's hush puppies from a paper sack. He put the fried cornbread into the oven to heat up.

On the coffee table in front of the sofa, we set up Siler's old cassette player and connected it to a wall outlet. A light the size of a pinhead turned green when we pressed the power switch. Pearl put the cassette into the machine, Side A facing out through the tiny window. We heard the tape chugalug when she pressed rewind.

"Might as well start at the beginning," she said.

The rewind function clicked off when it reached the start of the tape. At the same time, my phone buzzed. Sounded loud as thunder. A text from Miss Emmy. Said she would be in Chapel Hill that night and needed to meet with Pearl and me. Details forthcoming. I texted a thumbs-up emoji and put the phone away.

"Lassie, you should hit play," Ghost said. "H.F. asked you to produce the music for his memorial service. This one is yours."

My mind flew away, back to 1982. H.F. standing by a crepe myrtle on the lawn at He's Not Here, our Tuesday night bar, and reciting a speech about gravy he would deliver the next day in his public speaking course. He was tall, with muscled shoulders and arms. I could see him laughing at his own jokes about gravy. Beer sloshed over the lip of the blue cup in his hand. Young men and young women around him, fans and friends. His stringy hair suggested rock and roll. He winked at the moment his story ran from truth to fiction. I saw his eyes bright as the stars in the belt of Orion. I pressed play and said a silent prayer that his voice would come through the speakers.

We heard hissing. The antique tape spit and yawned and crackled and popped, giving us back the ambient sounds and muffled talk from an amateur recording of an amateur band trespassing in a campus building seven Mondays before Michael Jordan hit the shot that brought the University its first men's basketball national championship in a quarter-century.

Then, H.F.'s voice.

"Hello, hello, hello. One, two, three. This is Monday night, February 8th, 1982. Cane Creek band rehearsal. No, no. Scratch that. Snow Camp band rehearsal," H.F. said.

Then the voice of young Ghost. "Introduce the band, man."

"That's Ghost on bass," H.F. said, "and we have Delaney-Quinn on guitar. Yours truly, H.F. Turley, on lead vocals." There was a pause.

"You on drums," H.F. said. "What's your name?"

Delaney-Quinn's voice. She revealed the drummer's name and gave H.F. instructions.

"Yeah, and Delaney-Quinn on vocals, too. And Terrible Tim Creek on drums."

Tuning of instruments and bursts of sounds from warm-ups. Then three false starts on a song.

Finally, everybody was in sync, or nearly so, and H.F.'s singing came through the speakers.

Theology and trains,
only heaven knows the pain.
Stranded at the station,
praying that he'll call my name
and then praying that he won't, thank you just the same.

O Lord, don't let me drown in my grits.
I want to play steel, pedal not ammo.
I wanna take stages, from Raleigh to Waco.
Lord, don't let me die where I sit.
Don't let me pass out and drown in my grits.
Lord, don't let me die in my grits.
Don't let me die in my grits.

Singing those Porthole blues.
Chasing down the sun and moon.
Running out of time, running out of room.
Trying catch the angel,
before the devil gets to me

The song ended. We were quiet. Siler reached over and pressed the stop button on the player.

When Pearl saw the tears in my eyes, her eyes grew wet and reflected light. Delaney-Quinn laughed, and that started us all laughing. We laughed and cried at the same time. We missed H.F. We ate Siler's warmed-over hushpuppies off a hot tray. We toasted Snow Camp with fried cornbread. Chewed and laughed and wiped tears from our cheeks.

I served mugs of tea.

"Snow Camp lives," Delaney-Quinn said.

She pressed the play button. Long stretch of hissing. Clouds of sound. Then we heard Delaney-Quinn's voice. Her dirge.

CHAPTER TWENTY-THREE

On the Old Plank Road
say a prayer for these
wind grieved ghosts
who can't find peace

Chapped by cold
and the Cane Creek draw
souls are searching
up and down the Haw

Pray me home again
Down the Old Plank Road
Pray me home again
Down the Old Plank Road

The call has come
for me this night
Wrapped in wings
and wisdom's light

As I cross the river
I will comfort these
wind grieved ghosts
who can't find peace

Pray me home again
Down the Old Plank Road
Pray me home again
Down the Old Plank Road

Pray for all lost souls
Pray me back in time
Pray me cross the river
Lord, grant me peace of mind

Pray me home again
Down the Old Plank Road
Pray me home again
Down the Old Plank Road

Delaney-Quinn hit pause. She showed a look on her face that sought validation. Pearl clapped and declared Snow Camp worthy of the album we had all imagined the band would record way back when. Ghost agreed. He argued in favor of featuring the songs at H.F.'s memorial. Siler voted in the affirmative. Delaney-Quinn acknowledged the songs were better than she remembered.

"What about Lassie's song?" Pearl said. "Is that on here?"

"We shall see," Delaney-Quinn said as she hit play.

We let the tape run on through the rest of the recorded songs. Snow Camp got through all nine original tracks and a Rattlesnake Annie cover. Everybody liked the biscuit song. *I miss my biscuit baby, my flour power lady . . .*

We all laughed at Delaney-Quinn's song about her on-again, off-again romance with H.F.

I'm going to pinch your butt
I really, really must
I believe that this is lust
That is keeping us
Together

She laughed and winced at that one. Nine original tunes. Our dormmates played them all, start to finish. A monumental achievement for the rookie musicians steeling themselves for the band's big moment on the Springfest '82 bill.

Siler said he would close Pig Farm for rehearsals if the Green Gables guys would get together to learn the Snow Camp songs for H.F.'s service. Ghost used Siler's phone to make the phone call. He secured their commitment for Wednesday and Thursday afternoon band practice. Siler switched from tea to rye to celebrate the promise of new old music. Those of us who were un-pregnant joined him. Our collective consumption required the opening of a new bottle of Bulleit. Siler used the steak knife letter opener to cut the seal. Pearl offered Delaney-Quinn another night in the guest room.

I was reading a new text from Miss Emmy. She had to reschedule. Miss Emmy said she was tied up with federal men in dark suits. I told her Siler was closing Pig Farm on Wednesday for band practice. She agreed to meet us at the bar for a private meeting that morning.

"Hey, what happened to the guitar pick? Wasn't there a pick hidden in the cubby?" Delaney-Quinn said.

I went back to the countertop and shuffled barbecue sandwich wrappers and clamshells of banana pudding and paper trays of hushpuppies and slaw. I pulled the pick from a glob of pudding that settled as mortar in a vanilla wafer structure. I started to lick the pick. When Delaney-Quinn pushed a napkin between my mouth and the pudding pick, I wiped the thing clean.

It was an everyday black guitar pick. Thinnest outline of a logo was visible. I put the pick on the countertop and used the zoom setting on my camera phone to get a look.

I read out loud what I saw, "Parlier's Music Co."

"Not a clue," Ghost said. He was spending more time on Pearl's phone than Pearl. He stepped away to make a call.

I looked at Siler, who shook his head. Pearl shrugged. Delaney-Quinn asked me to spell out the wording, and she was zipping through search-engine results in no time. I put the pick in my pocket and found a spoon and an unopened clamshell of banana pudding. I ate from Miss Emmy's donated goods.

"You're not gonna believe this," Delaney-Quinn said.

"What? The pick is really a stock certificate?" Pearl said.

"Better," Delaney-Quinn said. She kept studying her screen. She'd gotten our attention. We watched her and waited for whatever was better than a fortune in stocks.

"A woman named Flossie Mae walked into Parlier's Music Company one day and bought her son a guitar. Bought him his first guitar. Flossie and her people were part of the Tom Joad migration," Delaney-Quinn said as she read from a web site.

"And?" Pearl said. "Let's hear it."

"Flossie Mae Haggard of Bakersfield, California, walked into Parlier's and bought her son Merle his first-ever guitar," Delaney-Quinn said.

"I guess Mama really tried," Siler said.

"And you damn near lose the pick in the banana pudding," Delaney-Quinn said. She gave me the same look I saw one night in the dorm when I ate her last slice of pizza. "I'm going to get that pick from you."

Ghost was on a borrowed phone working through a series of conversations. He had called in favors to book Forest Theatre for H.F.'s memorial service. We had the venue for next Sunday. That gave us seven days to organize a program. Minimal remarks. Emphasis on the music from Snow Camp's lost Springfest tapes. I had to figure out a way to get Delaney-Quinn to sing with the band.

"Tell you what, DQ," I said. "You play the Snow Camp show on Sunday, the Parlier's pick is yours."

Pearl, as always, was a step ahead. Before I'd finished my offer, she poured another glass of rye for Delaney-Quinn.

"I'll call my beet guy," Siler said. "You're not going to believe this tapenade."

Chapter Twenty-Four

WEDNESDAY, OCTOBER 16TH

Pearl kissed me awake.

Our bedroom was dark. Clouds concealed starlight. Pearl rolled on top of me and pressed her forehead against mine. I saw green eyes.

Pearl's gown was gone. She slid off my T-shirt and shorts. She lay still for a bit, her lips on mine. Her body on mine. Her legs on my legs. She kissed my cheek and my neck and whispered something in my ear. I couldn't make out what she said.

Pearl rocked her hips. She pointed her toes. She moved. She danced. She whispered in my ear again. This time, I heard the words. She was singing a song I wrote a couple of years back. She moved her lips and her hips.

> *I fly in through the window*
> *and wake you up with whiskey kisses.*
> *I wake you up with whiskey kisses.*

Pearl led the dance and made sure we finished the song together. She held her position. Her head found my shoulder. She fell asleep.

I faded in and out, dreams running through the folds of my brain as I felt Pearl's heart thump on my chest. I dreamed of Pearl stretched out in a cast iron bathtub at the little oyster bar on the intracoastal waterway, a gas station turned saloon outfitted with dozens of old tubs. Pearl waved me over to join her in the tub. We slid off the dock and into the water and floated toward stars. Sleep held us until Pearl kissed me awake for the second time that morning.

"Miss Emmy waits for no man," Pearl whispered in my ear.

She squeezed one last time and disappeared.

We got to Pig Farm by 10:30 that morning. We were ahead of Miss Emmy. Having chosen love over breakfast, genmaicha tea would have to hold us.

Miss Emmy arrived wearing an unwrinkled blue suit and concern on her face. We had been seated in our usual spot, at the end of the bar closest to the entrance. With Siler in position. Leaning his right elbow on the bar. Coffee in his left hand. Miss Emmy waved to Siler and walked past us, calling us down to the far end of the bar. She moved a barstool to the corner and pointed Pearl and me to seats on either side.

Siler delivered coffee to Miss Emmy and returned to his usual post. Miss Emmy spoke in a quiet voice.

"What the fuck did you two think you were doing?" she said. "My influence has limits, mind you. Out of some fires I cannot pull your asses."

Pearl looked at me. I had nothing. This wasn't making any sense. Miss Emmy saw puzzles on our faces.

"Corn Stalks, goddamnit. The boys from Langley have been proctologically involved in my life the past week," Miss Emmy said.

Pearl lost color in her face. I shook my head. Miss Emmy saw no feint, no bluff.

"Oh, no," she said. "I should have given my honeybun more credit."

Miss Emmy made a motion with her hand that Siler understood to be a call for whiskey. Siler poured whiskey for me and Miss Emmy. Pearl took the bubbly water with lime. When Siler started to walk back to the other end of the bar, Miss Emmy tilted her head in a direction that let him know he could stay and listen in.

"So, Pauley and FBI are still investigating?" Pearl said.

Miss Emmy shook her head. Pauley and the FBI were out of the picture, as far as she could tell. Same for the state investigators. Another three-letter federal agency was running things.

"Their badges say State Department and Homeland Security," Miss Emmy said, "but their suits and their sense of humor say otherwise. Or lack of sense of humor, I should say. These boys stick to national security questions. They want to know people's secrets. There's no real murder investigating going on, at least not the usual kind."

Siler held his expression.

"Why us?" Pearl said. She knew the answer as soon as the words left her lips.

"Because you two tried to kill the idiots once. Seems like you'd keep going 'til you got it right," she said. "Where I come from, you put a gun in a man's neck that's a sure sign you're ready to take his life."

Pearl shook her head. I focused on my breathing.

Miss Emmy drank a gulp of whiskey and winced at the sting. She looked at Pearl, then looked at me.

"Honeybun, it's not Langley sniffing your trouser leg. It's yours truly.

Death has so swallowed up your lives in the last year. I figured, what's one more death to Lassie James. What's one more lie," Miss Emmy said. "Sometimes I forget that my chosen profession doesn't account for sentiment."

Miss Emmy explained that the suits from Langley were going through all the paper files in her office and downloading data and email from every server and every desktop. She said they even had a way to download images of items that her staff had passed through the copy machines.

"I tell you, honeybun. Inside these men beat cold, cold hearts," she said. "Their eyes are trained on anything that hints to China. There are no hymns inside these men."

Doll, she said, was telling everything she knew. Which was not a lot. Doll knew nothing of foreign agents. Doll had seen dollar signs and said yes to anything that put money into her accounts. She had been the easiest of easy marks for the agents of China hoping to swing the election her way in exchange for a puppet governor and the chance to extract lithium and rare earth elements. Doll was revealing every detail about payments. She knew nothing about land deals or lithium. She knew account balances.

Miss Emmy told us we were wrong in assuming SKO was a front for Chinese agents in land transactions with the University. Just the opposite. With Congress having passed the CHIPS Act and considering additional legislation, she described the new river of U.S. money available to back the on-shoring of technology manufacturing. The policies were designed to loosen China's hold on technologies deemed critical to U.S. national security. With Leander's outreach, the SKO deal got the immediate green light because it pulled in U.S. investors and U.S. manufacturers. Thanks to Leander, it would be U.S. firms, not China, extracting lithium from Caldwell County and from the land in Montana. Or rare earth minerals if they could find them. In turn, if the mines did not give up treasure, it would be U.S. investors repurposing the land into pig farms or some other cash-rich operation.

"Here's to the joy of being wrong," Siler said. He drank his whiskey glass dry and poured more for the three of us.

Thanks to Leander, SKO had ties to Langley. Leander was well positioned to be a source for intel. Made sense.

"Some real *Good Shepherd* shit. Damned if we're not all boot makers to kings," Siler said.

Siler was in the position. Dumb look on his face. Miss Emmy nodded and reached out to touch his arm. Sexy indifference, for sure.

"Boot makers don't wear greed too well, sweetheart. Or for too long," Miss Emmy said. "Corn Stalks threw Battle Park into the mix to run up their fees. Jackleg distillery idea. Got greedy for cash money, those two. Got greedy for fame, for celebrity. The China snoops saw it. And they spotted Langley in their rearview mirror at the same instance they saw Corn Stalks dancing on the six o'clock news. The China snoops wanted a quiet, anonymous front that would cover up their grab. Then they saw they had greedy clowns attracting attention."

Doll was lucky to get out alive. The upstart political party backing her, THAI, was dead and buried. News reports credited the FBI with the investigation and arrests and seizure of assets. Miss Emmy said it was Langley putting THAI out of business.

Russian and Chinese groups, through a series of shell companies and nonprofits, had been filling THAI accounts. Just like Russian and Chinese bots dominated the THAI social media accounts. Net result was a bunch of human North Carolina voters were abiding instructions generated by foreign robots communicating through social media channels. It was robots sending voters the click-to-donate links. Robots were also talking to robots. Foreign agents had programmed robot shell companies to tell other robot accounts when to click and donate foreign funds to Doll's campaign.

"Robots laundering money through links that were trending because lots of robots followed them," Miss Emmy said.

Hearing that, Pearl flung her phone across the bar.

From what Miss Emmy gathered, Langley described this as the beginning, not the end, of the foreign attempts to manipulate U.S. elections and to extract U.S. natural resources. China wouldn't view the death of THAI and the death of Corn Stalks as a failure. A trial run, nothing more. Killing Corn Stalks was as easy as dumping a souffle that didn't rise. Wipe the pan and try again. Use lessons from the trial run to get better results next go round.

"They don't come right out and say it," Miss Emmy said. "I can tell from the way the Langley boys talk about it. Corn Stalks died a god-awful death. Poison. They say the Chinese are experts at death by poison. The suits went on and on about Heartbreak Grass. Poison from some kind of vine. Assassins use it. Honeybun, go use your machine to find a billionaire named Long something. Killers hid the poison in his cat stew. Cat fucking stew."

Miss Emmy kept talking. She heard Langley boys mention deadly berries. Heard agents discussing chinaberry poisoning. Heard the agents talking about belladona, or nightshade.

"The poison that killed Juliet," Miss Emmy said. "The Langley men talked like China's agents have expertise with these plants. I'm sure the Langley boys do, too."

CHAPTER TWENTY-FOUR

A chill ran from my neck down my arms.

"The other night I had a dream," I said.

I described the dream about the train, about sitting in the dining car with Pearl. Famous twosomes all around us.

"Pearl and I were drinking champagne. There was a song playing. A Lumineers song. I remember it now. The song is called 'Nightshade.'"

Everyone was silent for a bit.

Miss Emmy said she hadn't seen an autopsy report. She repeated what she said earlier. The agents showed no interest in Corn Stalks.

"Whatever they believe, there will be no day in court. No public airing," Miss Emmy said. "You could toss water on those boys, and they wouldn't admit hydrogen talks to oxygen."

The agents cared about the communication channels Corn Stalks used, not their deaths. Langley cared about the Corn Stalks connections to Swan Valley and CAC. Langley cared about how those two firms created and maintained open lines to U.S. elected officials and candidates for office.

"I'd like to think it's one man, one vote here in the U.S. of A.," Miss Emmy said. "I'm starting to worry it's one man, one vote and whatever Beijing adds to the tally."

Siler's phone buzzed. A text from the Green Gables guys. They'd arrived to rehearse and found the front door locked. We offered to assist Miss Emmy with an exit down the back stairs. She surprised us by asking to stay for the Green Gables session. She called her staff and told Eugenia to clear her afternoon appointments.

"Honeybun, six billion people on the planet. The only ones I want to see right now are you folks and the Gables fellows playing the lost Springfest tapes live and in person," she said.

Siler had not had time to pick up the usual supply of sandwiches. Miss Emmy called Eugenia back and asked her to send a car over to Philpot Lane and deliver the goods to Pig Farm.

As the Green Gables boys loaded in, I texted Delaney-Quinn and begged her to come over and rehearse. We needed her Sunday to recreate the Snow Camp songs for H.F.'s memorial service. She sang lead on "Plank Road," "Bad Haircut," "Mansion" and "Mama Was Right About You." I told her I'd throw in the Parlier's pick. As she'd done in response to my previous pleadings, Delaney-Quinn sent back a thumbs-down emoji.

"Honeybun, you give me her number," Miss Emmy said. "I'll send a state trooper to fetch your singer."

Chapter Twenty-Five

SUNDAY, OCTOBER 20TH

By door knocking the neighborhood and talking up her recycle campaign at Pig Farm, Pearl had 29 old cell phones to recycle.

"Copper, lithium, aluminum, gold, carbon, glass and other stuff extracted from soil and oil," Pearl said. "All back in circulation."

She took her phone, the one she bounced off the Pig Farm wall, and tossed it into the box on our kitchen table.

"Let's make it 30," she said.

The facility handling electronics recycling would be open Monday. Pearl would deliver the box tomorrow, diverting plastics, circuit boards, batteries and liquid crystal displays from the landfill and, she believed, to some virtuous repurposed use.

"No more phone for you?" I said. "Whose phone is Ghost going to borrow?"

"You have no idea," she said. "Joansie found his cell and gave it to me to recycle."

As for Pearl's connectivity, she'd worked out a way to run phone calls through her laptop computer. Her plan was to dump the phone and keep the computer.

"And when you don't have the laptop with you?" I said.

"Then I'll survive the way you did in 1982," she said. "That was the loveliest part of our little hypnosis experiment. Hearing you describe a day in your 1982 life. You never referred to anyone checking their phone. Or missing a call. Or making a call. Somehow you all figured out how to meet up at The Upper Deck. Figured out how to organize a band rehearsal. You figured out how to get to the Cradle for a show."

"I like it," I said. "You're rolling back your digital footprint to the '80s."

"And you figured out how to get to Troll's to kiss Delaney-Quinn," Pearl said. "So I know you'll figure out how to track me down."

We were on barstools at the breakfast spot off the kitchen. Pearl finished her breakfast. She stood up and wiped her hands on the back pockets of her jeans. I tasted salty pork when she kissed me on her way upstairs to change for H.F.'s memorial. She accepted my encouragement to go casual. She'd keep the jeans and put on a cotton cable sweater.

Rain had slowed at sunrise and finished soon after. Weather was mild. Stone pews at Forest Theatre would be wet. Temperatures easy to manage. I'd seen Green Gables through their two days of rehearsals. The lost Springfest tapes sounded promising. Delaney-Quinn answered the governor's call to appear at Pig Farm to practice. Her singing voice was better than I remembered. Now, as then, she was our star.

Siler texted to report his beet guy had come through. We would memorialize H.F. with a local seasonal menu, as he directed in his will.

Toasted pita chips from a Calvander bakery. Beet tapenade from Siler's beet guy in Efland. Something with grilled brussels sprouts and goat cheese from a Raleigh chef. Pepper jelly and cream cheese dip from a farm stand in Asheboro.

"And Sunrise ham biscuits," Siler added in a final text on menu.

"See you at noon," I wrote back.

We'd agreed on the program. Ghost would welcome everyone and introduce me. I drafted remarks that honored H.F.'s request for speeches not to exceed the length of Lincoln's second inagural. I wrote out 539 words. That gave a little cushion for Ghost's welcome remarks and Delaney-Quinn's introduction of the music from Snow Camp's lost Springfest tapes.

As I wrote, it hit me that this was my first eulogy. I'd written obituaries and stories of death and stories of catastrophe. This would be my first time writing and delivering words at a memorial service. We had no service for Mom and Dad. Only the obituary I wrote about their lives. There was a short graveside service for Pearl's dad. I didn't speak. Now I was writing and speaking about a guy I knew so well so long ago. A guy I hadn't seen in years.

At Forest Theatre, early arrivers made plates of food. Siler had set up a serving table in the space between the stage and the first stone pew. Stage right. Ghost welcomed everyone and gave me the mic. H.F.'s service marked my first time on the Forest Theatre stage. I stepped onto the Chapel Hill gravel and looked out at the 22 stone pews. In my mind I was seeing the 1937 photograph of the place. Before masons built the pews. Before there was anything but a single line of stones marking the breakpoint between the audience on the grassy hillside and performers on the stage. I was occupying a spot held by speakers and performers for more than 100 years.

For H.F., friends covered about one-third of the amphitheater. I could see Delaney-Quinn and the Green Gables guys. All on the first stone pew. Ghost took a seat alongside the band members. I saw faculty members

I knew. I saw strangers. Up at the top, at the end of the last pew beside the old tree growing out of a circle of stones, I saw Siler. Miss Emmy was seated to his right. I believed they were holding hands. He whispered something to her. She laughed. She whispered something to him. His expression remained unchanged.

Midway up the rows, center aisle, I saw Pearl. She wore a floppy gold hat, something between a beanie and a beret. My throat tightened. Lord, help me. How I loved that woman. The stone pews were wet. She had a folded blanket under her rump. She lit up the air around her. I wasn't sure any words would come out when I started to speak about H.F. Pearl smiled. She waved. Excitement on her face, like it was the first time she'd seen me in months. I said a secret prayer wishing to be the one to die first.

I said out loud the words I had written down about H.F.

H.F. Turley was a beautiful man. Since his passing, I have been day-dreaming about him, about the early 1980s man I knew. I was lucky to know him then. I am thankful he comes to me now in my dreams.

My friendship with H.F. was one of extremes. For a few years in the early 1980s, I knew him in the intimate way we knew dormmates. The way we knew people before central air conditioning caused us to close our doors and windows. Then for several decades, I had little contact with him. Such extremes, I believe, draw us into mythmaking. H.F. was and is a mythical figure to me. He's forever the beautiful man with stringy rock-and-roll hair and the muscles of a farmer. And a big blue cup in his hand.

In my imagination, H.F. also created a mythology of those years we spent together in and around Connor Dorm. He must have built up myths, given what he asked us to do here today.

In his farmhouse in Sparta, H.F. had a shelf of books filled with Zen prayers and meditations. Ghost passed along a few of these to me. In one of the books, I saw H.F. had highlighted a Zen proverb:

"Before enlightenment chop wood, carry water. After enlightenment chop wood, carry water."

In the Zen book, by the way, H.F. had used the same kind of blue highlighter he used in the old days. A hundred thousand yellow highlighters on campus, and H.F. chose blue. I remember him saying his highlighter made the important sections of his books look like the morning sky.

For most of us, the years on this campus turned out to be our period of enlightenment. A few of us were wise enough to know it at the time. Others, myself included, understood it once we left this place and saw how dark the world could be. Maybe some of us only understand the light once we have walked through darkness.

H.F. was strong and sweet. He could be charming. He could be a nuisance. He believed in Snow Camp. He believed in the songs we wrote, the songs he sang, the songs you'll hear today.

H.F. could talk. More than once, I was with him at He's Not Here when he spent the evening drinking beer from a blue cup and rehearsing the speech he was going to deliver the next day in class.

When we left Connor Dorm and made our way in the world, we had no idea what we'd become. It was as if a slingshot had flung us out into the world. Ghost was the bass player who became a lawyer. Delaney-Quinn the guitar player and singer who became a doctor. H.F. took another turn. He moved to Sparta and became a farmer.

He gave speeches and sang lead in the band on his way to enlighten-ment. After enlightenment, he farmed trout and sold the fish to fancy restaurants. He grew Christmas trees around which families prayed and played.

He chopped wood and carried water. I'd like to think he kept singing. A singing farmer who left an eight-pound Ludell maul stuck in a sweetgum log and left his land to the Cherokee.

That was it. I was never any good at writing endings. I just stopped. There was a moment of uncertainty and silence. Folks were unsure if the eulogy was over. It was. I walked up center aisle and sat beside Pearl, grateful to be in her glow.

Delaney-Quinn took the stage. She took my spot on the Chapel Hill gravel. She introduced the Green Gables guys. She wore jeans and an ancient Spanky's bar sweatshirt. She told the Snow Camp origin story. This surely put us over H.F.'s word count. Maybe because it was coming from the band, this counted as music. Either way, no eulogy police appeared.

It was fall of 1981, Delaney-Quinn said, and she and Ghost and H.F. were getting stoned and watching "All My Children" on the TV in the dorm lounge. They were caught up in the spat between young lovers Greg Nelson, Liza Colby and Jenny. They each argued on behalf of a different character in the soap saga. Their round-robin debate took a turn. Their lines, they believed, were worthy of a song. Together, they started crafting an original tune about the highs and lows of life in Pine Valley. Which led them to conclude they should start a band. They dropped the Pine Valley song and worked on naming the band. And Snow Camp was born.

As her own memorial to H.F., Delaney-Quinn lit up a joint right there on stage. She took a puff. She talked about how much she wished one of them had held onto the lyrics from that first song, "Pine Valley Blues." Instead, our treasure hunt had turned up nine songs from Snow Camp's lost Springfest tapes. She pinched the fire out of the joint and tucked it behind her ear.

From the right front pocket of her jeans, Delaney-Quinn pulled out the Parlier's pick. She put the pick to her lips and gave it a kiss. Then she hollered out the count, and the band kicked off the memorial show with her love song to H.F., "$2 and a Bad Haircut."

The band closed with "My Biscuit Baby." Everybody sang. Pearl squeezed my hand.

"Little Bougainvillea Battle is tapping her feet," she whispered in my ear.

Chapter Twenty-Six

There was no encore. Snow Camp's lost Springfest tapes included nine songs and only nine. Nobody knew the Rattlesnake Annie cover.

From the Forest Theatre stage, Delaney-Quinn offered a benediction. Took the joint from behind her ear and lit it again. And we were done. Ghost gave an executor's nod, affirming we had satisfied the wishes H.F. set forth in his will.

Ghost and Delaney-Quinn headed out with the Green Gables band members for the walk to Pig Farm.

Siler, Miss Emmy, Pearl and I were the last ones left in the stone amphitheater. Miss Emmy asked Pearl about her hat. Siler dumped ice from coolers. Miss Emmy had wiped clean her calendar again and said she'd head back to Pig Farm with us.

When I said I wanted to hang back and talk with Siler a minute, Pearl and Miss Emmy headed out toward Battle Lane for the walk to the bar. Pearl took off her hat and gave it to Miss Emmy to wear. Pearl toted a sack of ham biscuits.

Siler and I started down the OWASA trail into the Battle Park woods.

"From the grave, H.F. gave us a bunch of gifts," Siler said.

He was right about that. Gifts from the grave. But for H.F.'s passing and his request to have us play the Snow Camp songs at his service, we would never have rediscovered the music. We never would have renewed our friendship with Delaney-Quinn. I never would have taken possession of stock worth $1.3 million. I was thinking Siler would not have been holding hands with Miss Emmy. But for H.F., Delaney-Quinn wouldn't have the Parlier's pick.

"We chop wood and carry water," I said. "We're lucky if we get to chop wood and carry water alongside friends."

We approached the rock terrace and stopped to stare into the woods. Sat on stone benches. It was a day for stone.

"I've been thinking about what Miss Emmy said the other day, about the boys from Langley talking about heartbreak grass, about china-berry and nightshade," I said.

Siler's expression was unchanged.

"When Dr. Biocca's report came back with news about the wood pulp in Miss Emmy's pig, I started reading all kinds of horror stories about processed food. The wood pulp seems harmless. Other stuff, though. Read about McDonald's recalling 12 million promotional drinking glasses back in 2010. Glasses with pictures of cartoon characters," I said. "No wood pulp. It was cadmium. Traces of cadmium. About the same time Walmart got dinged for selling children's jewelry that contained cadmium. Apparently, cadmium is bad stuff."

From the rock terrace, Siler started up Solitary Hill Trail. It would carry us for a short loop around to Bent Beech Trail. I followed.

"Yeah," Siler said. "Hearing Miss Emmy talk about the poisons reminded me of that old movie, the one you invited me to watch in the library.

One of the British films you had to watch for an RTVMP class."

My undergraduate major—radio, television and motion pictures—guaranteed me the chance to watch movies all day. No matter the University did away with the major not long after I took the degree. Siler's question prompted me to recall the excitement of watching movies while my dormmates were taking tests.

"*White Cargo?* The one from the Ida Simonton novel?" I said.

That wasn't it. We walked farther.

"It was *The Twickenham Sisters,*" Siler said. "Early '40s. I found it streaming a couple of months back."

Siler summarized the movie. Two sisters grow up poor as dirt in east London. Dickensian lives. The younger Twickenham sister is a stunning beauty. She marries a wealthy shipowner and cashes in. She offers her older sister employment. Offers to hire her as a domestic worker in her mansion. Older sister needs the money and takes the job. No surprise, older sister grows to despise younger sister. She also starts an affair with the shipowner. While she doesn't possess her younger sister's beauty, she brings unusual enthusiasm into the bedroom.

"Then the older sister figures out a way to coat the inside of a teacup with poison," I said. "When the shipowner pours his wife a cup of tea one afternoon, he murders her. And the older sister swoops in to marry. A maid washes the dishes, and all evidence is down the drain."

"Yep, that's the one," Siler said. "Poison is a funny thing."

He navigated trails across Battle Branch Creek and past the Old Poplar Picnic Place and up a hill to Rainy Day Trail. Clouds that had dispersed for H.F.'s service were reorganizing. We felt drops.

"Hearing your eulogy today for H.F. Your words reminded me that I don't want to wait until you're gone to say my words," Siler said. "For forty years, our friendship has brought so many blessings to my life. Like the house up the hill there on Gimghoul. You gifting me and Carla the house has been a wonderful thing. I've been in these woods every day now for a year or more. The judge was right. If Pearl hadn't put a gun into Stokes, one of us would have."

He was quiet as we walked.

"I would have," he said.

The rain fell harder. We turned onto Deer Track Trail, which would take us to Sourwood Loop and to Park Place, where our route to Pig Farm would carry us past the arboretum's whiskey barrel artwork. Onward to see old friends, onward to a toast for H.F. I was curious to see who'd be wearing the floppy gold hat.

"Take this tree," Siler said. "Thanks to you gifting me the Gimghoul house, I've gotten to know these trees. This one is worth a look."

He picked up a stick and tapped the trunk of a tree.

"Lovely yellow leaves," I said. "About the color of Pearl's hat."

"Yeah," Siler said. "Pretty yellow leaves. See the berries. Turning red to black this time of year. Close your eyes and take a deep breath. You may get a scent from this tree."

I closed my eyes. I got the scent of the woods, the dead leaves, the petrichor from the raindrops.

"We could gather up these berries and make wine or jelly. Some folks say you can make cough syrup from this tree," Siler said. "But you take the leaves and seeds. The wood and the bark. Grind it all up and reduce it down. Like a demitasse. And you've got something a Chinese assassin would use. Might smell like almonds. And the hydrocyanic acid might kill somebody."

Siler flung the stick into the woods and kept walking.

"Prunus serotina," Siler said.

The rain had soaked us.

"Wild rum cherry," he said.

"Poison is a funny thing," I said.

Siler walked on, a few steps ahead of me. We were alongside Battle Branch Creek again, making the turn toward Forest Theatre and Park Place. We could hear crows cawing.

Siler was quiet.

"Congratulations on the, well, whatever the thing is with Miss Emmy," I said. "I'm glad she appreciates your sexy indifference as much as the rest of us do. As much as I have for forty-something years."

Siler told me Carla had confirmed she was ready to call it quits, this time for good. Third strike. She had informed him that she was seeing somebody. There was pain in his voice. Nobody is indifferent to the pain of a break-up. Nobody is indifferent to love. And experiencing love, we are always on the edge of pain. I changed the subject.

"Thank you for the kind words," I said. "I appreciate you speaking up before my eulogy. It's nice to hear it when I'm above ground."

We were back at Forest Theatre. Walked out onto the stage together. Alone among the stones and gravel and a century's worth of secrets. Siler pulled a flask from his jacket and took a swallow. He poured a drink onto the gravel for H.F. I could smell the rye. Always prepared, Siler. A crafty man. He passed me the flask.

"You are a smart guy, Siler," I said. "I've always known it. One of the smartest people I know. Are you really smart enough to have cooked up a wild rum cherry poison drink or a heartbreak grass cocktail? Or a shot of nightshade?"

Siler held his expression. No reaction. I drank two swallows of whiskey.

"Are you really smart enough to pull off the Twickenham trick? Smart enough to line highball glasses with poison and serve it to Corn Stalks? All the while managing to avoid harming yourself or anyone else coming near your bar glasses? Are you really that smart?" I said.

I passed the flask back to him. He took a drink.

"Nah," he said. "That would require more brainpower than I have. I'm not that smart."

He took a third swallow. Pocketed the flask. Gripped my shoulder and steered us toward Park Place for the rainy walk to Pig Farm. We walked by Battle Grove, the extraordinary stream restoration project that had given new life to a corner of campus that was a barren moonscape in the old days.

Siler picked up a stone from Battle Lane and tossed it into the stream.

"I'm not that smart," he said. "I am that indifferent."

Epilogue

In January when the ultrasound confirmed Bougainvillea Battle was tap dancing inside Pearl, Siler returned to the business of inventing mocktails. This time, his Bougainvillea Blues drink was a hit.

Siler left out the egg white and mixed Curacao syrup, lemon juice and Pellegrino. He added drops of sweet almond oil. Siler claimed he had the oil flown in from a family farm in the Deccan Plateau of India.

After he opened Pig Farm weekday mornings for Pearl and me and our Lamaze classmates, Siler took on fame as a mocktail shaman. All of the couples in the Lamaze classes demanded mocktails carrying the names they had picked out for the to-be children. Several rented out Pig Farm for gender reveal parties, using Siler's pink and blue mocktail concoctions to tease and ultimately reveal whether their unborn child carried a penis or vagina.

Pig Farm gained a flash of fame from the news coverage of our wacka-doo Saturday night selling chances to guess the combination to the old Fischer safe. Bars from Barstow to Bangor turned our safecracking challenge into a regular drinking game during the week, alongside their trivia nights. Turned out lots of people owned old safes and didn't know the combinations. These owners rented out the safes to neighborhood bars, turning white elephants into cash cows and, they hoped, rediscovering the combinations. State lottery commissions in Rhode

Island and Arizona that operated SafeCracker scratch-off games sued bars to prevent drinkers from gambling away their rent money with anyone other than their state government.

Pearl's electronics recycling enterprise grew into a little nonprofit business. She called it Cultured Pearls. By the spring equinox, she'd rounded up nearly a thousand old cell phones. Pearl chose her own algorithm for virtue. Said she'd consider getting a new cell phone once she had recycled ten thousand old phones. That sounded about right.

"Banking ten thousand selfless acts before one selfish act," I said. "Your dad would approve."

Pearl was practicing the alma mater on her psaltery. She would be ready to perform. R&R invited us to join him for music on the second Saturday in April, the date on the calendar we always marked for Springfest. That was long ago. I'd been dreaming about the long ago more and more. About the old days that for many years sped away from me. As the years clipped along, the old days with Ghost, H.F. and Delaney-Quinn fell farther away, farther into my past. Now things seemed to be coming around again. The old days seemed to be growing closer, as if my college years were riding on a sun that had left me and run its course halfway around the world and, just now, was starting to circle back toward me.

As the past drew closer to me, I felt the warmth of old friends. I kissed Pearl's lips and her tummy and day by day moved closer to a time I would be walking with Bougainvillea on the Battle Park trails. I kept praying my secret prayer to die before Pearl, to leave her earth before she left mine. Now I complicated the prayers by wishing to spend years with Bougainvillea and still find some way to predecease my Pearl. One day on a hike Pearl lay down on a cold rock slab alongside Battle Branch and invited me to rest beside her. She rolled into my arm and put her head on my shoulder and sang to me.

Pearl was vital. With Bougainvillea on the way, I decided I needed to discover a new commitment to improving my own health. When the doctor asked me whether I had considered becoming a vegetarian, I mumbled. The doc sighed. We sat in silence for a moment, the only sound in the room the crinkling of the paper underneath me on the examination table. Life is messy that way, filled with mumbles and sighs and crinkled truths.

Delaney-Quinn became a semi-regular at Pig Farm. She and Ghost found a producer in Lancaster, South Carolina, to turn the lost Springfest tapes into an album. The Green Gables guys joined Delaney-Quinn and Ghost in the studio. Siler put up money and founded Pig Farm Records. Ghost claimed listeners could smell the cannabis when they streamed the songs.

Doll landed in the same federal prison as Fats. A letter a month arrived from Fats. All sent to me in care of Pig Farm. All asking me to work with her on a movie script about our shared tale, the tale of our intimate friendship that ended when Fats killed Sanders Mallette and when Pearl arrived in Chapel Hill to bury her father and, yes, find me. Siler added each letter to the stack. I was praying we were done with death and memorial services and prison stories.

One March evening he handed me a package delivered to the bar. It was addressed to me.

"Not from Fats," he said.

It was a baby present. Inside the box was a cashmere onesie. The brightest, softest purple cashmere.

"Can babies wear cashmere?" Siler said.

There was a card.

"Congratulations, Lassie. I hope to meet your Pearl one day. You and she and me make three. Love, Darby. P.S. Love streaming your biscuit song."

"Oh, fuck," I said. "I'm going to need more rye to explain this one to Pearl."

I handed him the box to toss out. He felt weight in it. He pulled out a cell phone. Attached was an orange sticky note with writing that said "For Cultured Pearls." I pocketed the phone and would add it to my story for Pearl. I doubted Pearl would believe a truthful retelling of my night in Atlanta with Fats and Darby. An occasion for mumbles and sighs and crinkled truth, perhaps.

Siler poured. We drank. Siler told about visiting the Big Oak Drive-In with Miss Emmy to eat shrimp burgers in the coastal village of Salter Path. How the owner was so taken with Miss Emmy's celebrity that she offered to name a sandwich for the governor. Miss Emmy gushed with appreciation and thanked the woman and ultimately declined. Then Miss Emmy spoke up and said if the offer was still good, she'd appreciate the owner naming a sandwich for Pig Farm. And so now the Big Oak menu contains a Pig Farm pork sandwich.

"Thought you were going to say Miss Emmy had the lady name a sandwich Sexy Indifference," I said.

Siler smiled. He poured. He fiddled with the jukebox app and pulled up "All the Time in the World" from Secret Monkey Weekend. *Let's start with the clear blue skies . . .*

"I miss the days when we sat around Pig Farm doing nothing," Siler said. "I miss time."

He was behind the bar. In the position. A mug of coffee and a glass of rye in front of him. I'd had too many ryes by that point and concluded the only remedy was to have another. Maybe one or two more would give me an idea for explaining Darby to Pearl.

We spun classics through the juke, Fred Eaglesmith's "Alcohol and Pills," Loudon's "Dead Skunk," Lauderdale's "King of Broken Hearts," Guy Clark's "Dublin Blues." Twice I played my favorite Tom Waits song, "I Hope That I Don't Fall in Love With You." If Pearl and I were to have a song, I declared, this might be it.

Siler pre-empted my third spin by starting R.E.M.'s "Man on the Moon." Siler sang along, sang about Twister and Risk and finding his lover in heaven if she could get past the front gate.

"Your song, for you and Miss Emmy?" I said

Siler didn't respond. Noodled with his phone. When R.E.M. finished singing, Siler invited Rodgers and Hammerstein to make a rare appearance inside his vintage speakers.

I am caught and I don't wanna run,
'Cause I'm havin' so much fun with honey bun!

Snow Camp

The Lost Springfest Tapes

Snow Camp 1982

H.F. Turley . . . . Lead Vocals (winner best hair)

Delaney-Quinn . . . . Guitar & Vocals (I have the best weed!)

Argus Peppers . . . . Bass (will never get out of chapel hill alive)

Various . . . . Drums (Terrible Tim Creek is pretty good)

Piccolo player Hurricane Denise appears on $2 and a Bad Haircut courtesy of Cobb Dorm.

Recording Studio. . . . . Siler is lining something up. He heard about a place in Winston-Salem.

Van Driver:. . . . . Lassie James

Official Cheese Straws for Snow Camp:. . . . . Lassie's Mom

Album cover art: . . . . Teri is working on something. Would be cool to have graveyard on cover.

Official rehearsal space is that room in Swain Hall fucking Porthole is gotta be the official restaurant of Snow Camp band.

~~Cane Creek~~   ~~Silk Hope~~   ~~Plainfield Friends~~

Some girl named Billie knocked on my door and said she is in Lassie's anthro class and she's looking for him. Remind me to give him the message.

One Leg Down the Hill
by H.F. Turley

I'm planting Christmas trees, one leg down the hill.
Sixteen hours away from home, and I am working still.

The sun is rising overhead, and the water pail is dry.
There's a long blue ridge above the trees, and it stretches to the sky.

I haven't lost Alicia yet, but I'm afraid the end is near.
I haven't reached the edge of the earth, but I believe I can see it from here.
I believe I can see it from here.

The mountain work will leave me weak, and food is days away.
I'm eating laughs and drinking tears, and dancing through the day.

I haven't lost Alicia yet, but I'm afraid the end is near.
I haven't reached the edge of the earth, but I believe I can see it from here.
I believe I can see it from here.

The sunset glitters through the pines, a long day finally ends.
The ragged A-frame shack is home, and dreams of her begin.

I haven't lost Alicia yet, but I'm afraid the end is near.
I haven't reached the edge of the earth, but I believe I can see it from here.
I believe I can see it from here.

Maggie Blue

by H.F. Turley

Maggie Blue
Maggie Blue
Lost in space
How do you do?

I miss your cabbage
I miss your wine
I miss your green eyes
I miss good times

Maggie Blue
Maggie Blue
The sun is rising
Where are you?

I miss your rhubarb
and your buttermilk pie
I miss your chow chow
and your chicken fried

Maggie Blue
Maggie Blue
I'm in Snow Camp
Where are you?

I miss your cookies
I miss your cream
I taste your cornbread
In my dreams

Maggie Blue
Maggie Blue
The Porthole's calling
Where are you?

I miss your bacon
and your Brunswick Stew
I miss your sizzle
and your hot sauce too

Maggie Blue
Maggie Blue
My water's boiling
Where are you?

Maggie Blue
Maggie Blue
My water's boiling
Where are you?

Don't Let Me Die in My Grits

By H.F. Turley

Breathing those Waffle House fumes.
Driving by the light of the moon.
Running out of time, running out of room.
Trying catch the angel
before the devil gets to me

O Lord, don't let me drown in my grits.
I want to meet stars, from movie and sky.
I wanna sail, I wanna fly.
Lord, don't let me die where I sit.
Don't let me pass out and drown in my grits.
Lord, don't let me die in my grits.
Don't let me drown in my grits.

Theology and trains,
only heaven knows the pain.
Stranded at the station,
praying that he'll call my name
and then praying that he won't, thank you just the same.

O Lord, don't let me drown in my grits.
I want to play steel, pedal not ammo.
I wanna take stages, from Raleigh to Waco.
Lord, don't let me die where I sit.
Don't let me pass out and drown in my grits.
Lord, don't let me die in my grits.
Don't let me die in my grits.

Singing those Porthole blues.
Chasing down the sun and moon.
Running out of time, running out of room.
Trying catch the angel,
before the devil gets to me

O Lord, don't let me drown in my grits.
I want to play steel, pedal not ammo.
I wanna take stages, from Raleigh to Waco.
Lord, don't let me die where I sit.
Don't let me pass out and drown in my grits.

All My Underwear's Dirty
by H.F. Turley

My buddy walked in from his girlfriend's place,
His eyes were glazed, and he wore a long face.

I thought she had ditched him, or maybe had snitched him,
He looked kinda blank.
His fate was tough, he took it rough,
He had just been by the bank.

And he cried:

All my underwear's dirty, and my fuel light's blinking.
I've got three dollar bills, I spent the rest drinking.
I've gone through my boxers, and my fuel light's blinking.
I've got three crinkled bills, and I gotta stop drinking.

So like Rip van Winkle he drifted away,
'til it all blows over, in his bed he would stay.
I found him a Snickers and let him dream.
And as I walked out the door, I could hear him sing.

All my underwear's dirty, and my fuel light's blinking.
I've got three lonely bills, I spent the rest drinking.
I've worn both sides, and my fuel light's bright.
I'll sleep 'til it's over, I'll sleep day and night.

All my underwear's dirty, and my fuel light's blinking.
I'll spend my last dime in some honky tonk drinking.

My Biscuit Baby

By Lassie James

She's the apple of my eye
I'd choose her over pie
She melts my Irish butter
I could never love another

I miss my biscuit baby
My flour power lady
A friend to saints and sinners
Up for breakfast, lunch or dinner
She rises on her own
She never makes me eat a scone
My flour power lady
Oh, I miss my biscuit baby

She responds to every knead
Never frets about the heat
Never backs down from a jam
Wipes gravy from my pans

Her shining golden crown
Heart soft like goosey down
A host to bacon, eggs and cheese
And a fan of honey bees

I miss my biscuit baby
My flour power lady
A friend to saints and sinners
Up for breakfast, lunch or dinner
She rises on her own
She never makes me eat a scone

My flour power lady
Oh, I miss my biscuit baby

Some defame her old school ways
Claim she has seen her butter days
But she just laughs at all of y'all
Counting your cholesterol

I miss my biscuit baby
My flour power lady
A friend to saints and sinners
Up for breakfast, lunch or dinner
She rises on her own

She never makes me eat a scone
My flour power lady

Mama Was Right About You
By Delaney-Quinn

Mama was right about you.
When I bragged about your pretty kisses,
she told me all that I was missing.
Mama was right about you.

When I talked about your dreamy eyes,
she shook her finger at all your lies.
I loved to ride in your fancy truck.
She promised me you'd bring bad luck.
Mama was right about you.

With a cigarette hanging on her lips,
and her do-right hands up on her hips,
from her beauty parlor crystal ball,
Mama made a list of all
the lousy things you'd do.
Mama was right about you.

Like the time you ran off with the waitress,
or when you took that money from the church.
The gutters rotted on your watch,
and you made my Daddy curse.
Mama was right about you.

I loved the way you wore those jeans,
your charisma bursting out the seams,
so I never saw the pain you'd bring,
once the denim frayed.
Mama was right about you.

With a cigarette hanging on her lips,
and her do-right hands up on her hips,
from her beauty parlor crystal ball,
Mama made a list of all
the lousy things you'd do.
Mama was right about you

Old Plank Road
By Delaney Quinn

On the Old Plank Road
say a prayer for these
wind grieved ghosts
who can't find peace

Chapped by cold
and the Cane Creek draw
souls are searching
up and down the Haw

Pray me home again
Down the Old Plank Road
Pray me home again
Down the Old Plank Road

The call has come
for me this night
Wrapped in wings
and wisdom's light

As I cross the river
I will comfort these
wind grieved ghosts
who can't find peace

Pray me home again
Down the Old Plank Road
Pray me home again
Down the Old Plank Road

Pray for all lost souls
Pray me back in time
Pray me cross the river
Lord, grant me peace of mind

Pray me home again
Down the Old Plank Road
Pray me home again
Down the Old Plank Road

My Dream House is Not a Mansion Anymore
By Delaney-Quinn

It's time to change the reel
On the movie of my life
It's time to define victory,
Being more than just a wife

The great big world is calling,
Water, sand and sky
A diamond is no anchor,
And neither is a guy

I'm gonna visit The Brown Palace
And wink at all the cowboys
Gonna watch the sun set at Lahaina
And shut out all the noise

My dream house I once fought for
is not a mansion anymore
It's a cage that cannot hold me
I leave a wreath upon the door

My dream house is not a mansion anymore
My dream house is not a mansion anymore

$2 and a Bad Haircut

You tell me that you love me
But then you can barely
Tie your shoes
So full of booze
Seems you want to lose
me
I hate how you lie with ease
And lose your keys
And misspell Lebanese

But then you have that face
That pretty, pretty face
With blue eyes spaced
Just so
And that Roman nose
And cherry Corvette lips
And rock-a-baby hips
That swing in 3/4 time
I wish that you were mine
And I wish you had more money
And knew which jokes were funny
And found a better barbershop
To stop
You
From going out in public
With a haircut so, so ugly
A haircut so, so ugly

Your haircut catastrophe
Makes that face look more pretty
That pretty, pretty face
I want to kiss your face
I want to slap your face
How can the human race
produce that perfect skin
on my idiot boyfriend
How can the gods above
Condemn me to love
You
When you only have two dollars
And a hair cost much more
And you are such a bore
At dinner parties with our friends
Who wonder how I lured you in
Because you have that pretty face
And Americans like faces
So they all think you're aces
And tell me that I'm blessed
And that I am such a mess
And I should criticize you less

I'm going to pinch your butt
I really, really must
I believe that this is lust
That is keeping us

Together
Because you have that pretty face
That pretty, pretty face
With blue eyes spaced
Just so
And that Roman nose
And cherry Corvette lips
And rock-a-baby hips
That swing in 3/4 time
I wish that you were mine

SNOW CAMP

H. F. Turley, Lead Vocals (BEST HAIR!)

Delaney-Quinn, Guitar + Vocals (Best Weed)

Argus Peppers, Bass GHOST!

VARIOUS, Drums (Terrible Tim Creek is pretty soot)

Hurricane Denise appears on #2 courtesy of Cobb Dorm (Piccolo)

Recording Studio — Siler heard about a place in Winston-Salem

Van Drive — Lassie James

Official Cheese Straws — Lassie's MOM

SWAIN HALL rehearsal space

fucking Pantha6 official restaurant of SnowCamp

ALBUM COVER ART — Teri is working on something ~~tombstone~~?

~~CANE CREEK~~
~~SILK HOPE~~
~~Plainfield Plants~~

*Hey, some girl named Billie knocked on my door and said she's in a class with Lassie and is looking for him. Remind me to tell him

ONE LEG DOWN the HILL
H. F.

I'm planting Christmas trees, one leg down the hill
Sixteen hours away from home, and I am working still.

The sun is rising overhead, and the water pail is dry.
There's a long blue ridge above the trees, and it
stretches to the sky.

(chorus)
I haven't lost Alicia yet, but I'm afraid the end is near.
I haven't reached the edge of the earth, but I believe I
can see it
from here.
I believe I can see it from here.

The mountain work will leave me weak and food is far away.
I'm eating laughs and drinking tears, and dancing through
the day.

(chorus)

The sunset slithers through the pines a long day finally
ends.
The ragged A-frame shack is home, and dreams
of her begin.

(chorus)

Maggie Blue
H.F.

Maggie Blue
Maggie Blue
Lost i spap
How do you do?

I miss you cabbage
I miss your wine
I miss your green eyes
I miss good time

Maggie Blue
Maggie Blue
The sun is rising
Where are you?

I miss your rhubarb
and your buttermilk pie
I miss your chow chow
and your chicken fried

Maggie Blue
Maggie Blue
I'm in Snow Camp
Where are you?

I miss you cookies
I miss your cream
I taste your cornbread
In my dreams

Maggie Blue
Maggie Blue
The Portholes calling
Where are you?

I miss you bacon
and your Brunswick stew
I miss you size 4
and your hot sauce too

Maggie Blue
Maggie Blue
My water's boiling
Where are you?
My water's boiling
Where are you?

Don't Let Me Die in My Grits
H.F.

Breathing those Waffle House fumes.
Driving by the light of the moon.
Running out of time, running out of room.
Trying to catch the angel
before the devil gets to me.

O Lord, don't let me die in my grits,
I want to meet stars from a velvet sky.
I wanna sail, I wanna fly.
Lord, don't let me die where I sit.
Don't let me pass out and die in my grits
Lord, don't let me die in my grits
Don't let me drown in my grits.

Theology and trains,
only heaven knows the pain.
Stranded at the station,
praying that he'll call my name
and then praying that he won't,
thank you just the
same.
soul.

O, Lord don't let me drown in my grits
I want to play steel, pedal not amp,
I wanna take stages, from Raleigh to Waco.
Lord, don't let me die, where I sit.
Don't let me pass out and die in my grits
Don't let me die in my grits
Lord, don't let me die in my grits
Don't let me die in my grits

Singing the
Porthole Blues
chasing down the sun
and the
moon
Running out of time,
running out of room
Trying to catch the angel
before the devil
gets to
me

O Lord, don't let me
drown in my grits
I want to play steel,
pedal not amp
I wanna take stages
from Raleigh Waco

Lord, don't let me
die where I sit

Don't let me pass out
and drown
in my grits

ALL My Underwear's Dirty

H.F.

My buddy walked in from his girlfriend's place.
His eyes were glazed, and he wore a long face.
I thought she had ditched him, or maybe had snitched him,
He looked kinda blank.
His face was tough, he took it rough
He had just been too the bank.

And he cried:

All my underwear's dirty, and my fuel light's blinking
I've got three dollar bills, I spent the rest drinkin'
I've gone through my boxers and my fuel light's blinking
I've got three crinkled bills and I gotta stop drinking

So like Rip Van Winkle he drifted away
'til it all slows down, in his bed he would stay.
I found him a Snickers and let him dream
As I walked out the door I could hear him sing.

All my underwear's dirty and my fuel light's blinking.
I've got three lonely bills I spent the rest drinking.
I've worn both sides, and my fuel light's bright
I'll sleep 'til it's over, I'll sleep day and night

All my underwear's dirty, and my fuel light's blinking
I'll spend my last dime in some honky tonk drinking.

MY BISCUIT BABY
Lassie James

She's the Apple of my eye
I would choose her over pie
She melts my Irish butter
I would never love another

I miss my biscuit baby
My flour power lady
A friend to saints and sinners
Up for breakfast, lunch or dinner
She rises on her own
She never makes me eat a scone
My flour power lady
O, I miss my biscuit baby

She responds to every knead
Never frets about the heat
Never backs down from a jam
Wipes gravy from my pans

Her shining golden crown
Her most soft like gooey dough
A ~~sefge host~~ to bacon, egg and cheese
And a fan of honey bees

(chorus)

Some defame her old-
school ways
Claim she has seen
her butter days
But she just laughs
at all of y'all
Counting your
cholesterol

(chorus)

Mama Was Right About You
DQ

Mama was right about you.
When I bragged about your pretty kisses,
she told me all that I was missing.
Mama was right about you.

When I talked about your dreamy eyes,
she shook her finger at all your lies.
I loved to ride in your fancy truck.
She promised me you'd bring bad luck.

Mama was right about you.

With a cigarette hang'g on her lips
and her do-right hands up on her lips
from her beauty parlor crystal ball,
Mama made a list of all
the lousy things you'd do.
Mama was right about you.

Like the time you ran off wit the waitress,
or when you took that money from the church.
The gutters rotted on your watch,
and you made my Daddy curse.

Mama was right about you.
I loved the way you wore that jeans
your charisma bursting out the seams
Iss I never saw the pain you'd bring
once the denim frayed.
Mama was right about you.

With a cigarette
hanging on her lips
and her do-right hands
up on her lips
from her beauty parlor
crystal ball
Mama made a listful
the lousy things you'd do.

Mama was right about you

Old Plank Road

D.Q.

On the Old Plank Road
say a prayer for these
wind grieved ghosts
who can't find peace

chapped by cold
ant the Cane Creek thaw
souls are searching
up at down the Haw

Pray me home again
Down the Old Plank Road
Pray me home again
Down the Old Plank Road

The call has came
for me this night
wrapped in wings
and Wisdom's light

As I cross the river
I will comfort these
wind grieved ghost
who can't find peace

Pray me home again
Down the Old Plank Road
Pray me home again
Down the Old Plank Road

Pray for all lost souls
Pray me back in time
Pray me cross the river
Lord grant me peace of mind

Pray me home again
Down the Old Plank Road
Pray me home again
Down the Old Plank Road

My Dream House is not a Mansion Anymore

D.Q.

It's time to chase the reel
On the movie of my life
It's time to to find victory
Being more than just a wife

The great big world is calling
Water, sand, and sky
A diamond is no anchor,
And neither is a guy

I'm gonna visit the Brown Palace
And wink at all the cowboys
Gonna watch the sun set at Lahaina
And shout out all the noise

My dream home I once fought for
is not a mansion anymore
It's a cage that cannot hold me
I leave a wreath upon the door

My dream house is not a mansion anymore
My dream house is not a mansion anymore

#2 and a Bad Haircut

D. Q.

You tell me that you love me
But then you can barely
Tie your shoes
So full of booze
Seems you want to lose

me
I hate seein you lie with ease
And lose your keys
And misspell beaneel

•
But then you have that face
That pretty, pretty face
With blue eyes spaced
Just so
And that Roman nose
And those chevy corvette <u>Lips</u>
And rock a baby hips
That swing i 3/4 time
I wish that you were nicer
And I wish you had more money
And knew which jokes were funny
And found a better barbers up
To stop

You
From sortgoin i public
With a haircut so, so ugly
A haircut so, so ugly

Your haircut catastrophe
Makes that face look more pretty
That pretty, pretty face
I just tokin you say
I want to slap your face

How can the human race
produce that perfect skin
On my idiot boyfriend
How can the gods above
Condum me to love

You
when you only have #2
And a haircut cost much more
Ant you are such a bore
At dinner parties with our friends
Who wonder how I loved you so
Because you have that pretty face
Ant Americans like faces
So they all think you're all g
Ant tell me that she blessed
Ant that al on such a nerd
And I should criticise you less

•
I'm goin to pinch your butt
I really, really must
I believe that this is best
That's keepin us
Together
Because you have that pretty face
That pretty, pretty face
With blue eyes, spaced
Just so
Ant that Roman nose
And Chevy corvette <u>Lips</u>
Ant rock a baby hips
That swing i 3/4 time
I wish that you were nicer

D.Q. ♡ H.F.

SNOW   CAMP

Acknowledgements

I am grateful to Gwenyfar Rohler at Old Books on Front Street in Wilmington, Kimberly Taws at The Country Bookshop in Southern Pines, Don Pinney at Sutton's in Chapel Hill, Stacy Hawks at The Writing Wall, Rachel Lewis Hilburn at CoastLine, Aaron Keck at WCHL, Bob Burtman at WHUP, Main Street Books in Davidson, the team at Quail Ridge Books in Raleigh, and Ted, Clara, and Flo at Wisdom House Books for supporting local writers. Conversations with Em Williams, Lynn Mohr, David Menconi, Laura Compton, Nehemiah Stewart, Nancy Finger, Carol Graham, Kavita Hall, Chris Stamey, Natalie Gilbert, Robert Waldinger, Echo Morris and Leah Buchan taught me more about Lassie James. I've been lucky to have Don Dixon, Katharine Whalen, Clint Burgess, Steve Ferguson, Rod Abernethy, Jefferson Hart, Steven Tepper, Jana Collins, Trey Wilson, Gayle Murrell, Yung Nay, Pamela McLamb, Mandey Brown at Imbibe, and Kirk and Jody at The Kraken bring Pig Farm Tavern to life. Kendall Page's research revealed to me 200-plus years of Battle Park's secrets. Dave Schmidt, Margot Lester and Penny McPhee are readers whose touches make things better. Mom and Dad and Amy and Laura created a home where books mattered. Betsy, I miss you.

About the Author

John Bare is a writer and photographer. He is the author of the 2021 mystery, *Fair-Skinned Brunette with the Porcelain Shine*, which introduced Lassie James. With Don Dixon, John co-wrote songs for the 2019 album *Lassie James Songbook Vol. I*, a collection of twelve original songs supporting the Lassie James mystery series, and the 2023 album *Snow Camp 1982: The Long Springfest Tapes,* a companion to *My Biscuit Baby*. John was born in Winston-Salem and attended public schools in Garner, NC, where his parents were educators. He majored in radio, television and motion pictures at the University of North Carolina and later received a PhD in mass communication research from UNC. In Chapel Hill, he developed an appreciation for biscuits, whiskey, and live music. John shares his North Carolina house with rescue dogs Winston and Isadora. To follow the Lassie James series and to stay in touch with John, visit www.JohnBareBooks.com.

Printed in the USA
CPSIA information can be obtained
at www.ICGtesting.com
JSHW022345291123
52808JS00004B/17